CHRONICLE OF SAN GABRIEL

CHRONICLE OF SAN GABRIEL

by
JULIO RAMÓN RIBEYRO

Translated by
JOHN PENUEL

LATIN AMERICAN LITERARY REVIEW PRESS
Series: Discoveries
Pittsburgh, Pennsylvania
2004

The Latin American Literary Review Press publishes Latin American
creative writing under the series title *Discoveries*, and critical works
under the series title *Explorations.*

NATIONAL
ENDOWMENT
FOR THE ARTS

Acknowledgements
This project is supported in part by grants from
the National Endowment for the Arts in Washington D.C.,
a federal agency, and the
Commonwealth of Pennsylvania Council on the Arts.

PENNSYLVANIA
COUNCIL
ON THE
ARTS

Translation © Copyright 2004 by Latin American Literary Review Press
and John Penuel
Cover by David Wallace

Library of Congress Catalog-in-Publication Data

Ribeyro, Julio Ramón, 1929-
   [Crónica de San Gabriel. English]
   Chronicle of San Gabriel / by Julio Ramón Ribeyro; translated
   by John Penuel.
      p. cm.—(Discoveries)
   ISBN 1-891270-19-2 (alk. paper)
   I. Title. II. Series.
PQ8497.R47C713 2004
663' .64—dc22

                            2004001406

*To Mimí and the great summer days
in the "Viejo Dios."*

On *Chronicle of San Gabriel*

Chronicle of San Gabriel, my first novel, was written at the beginning of 1956, in Munich, when I was twenty-six years old. I had just arrived in Germany, didn't know German, and the hard winter (thirty-one degrees Celsius below zero, and the streets under a meter of snow) forced me to remain confined to the room I had rented in the suburban house of a working-class family.

The loneliness, lack of communication, and boredom soon became unbearable, and I saw no other remedy for my depression but to escape that reality through the imagination. So I opened a notebook and started writing the first thing that came to mind, the memories of a vacation I had spent on an Andean hacienda when I was fourteen or fifteen years old.

After a few days I was so absorbed by my work that I lost contact with everything around me. That absorption is perhaps why I wrote the book so quickly, for I am a rather slow writer who tends to work in fits and starts. It is one of the few experiences I have had of finding myself in a sort of "second state" while writing, so much so that what I was describing seemed to me the real world and reality a world read or dreamed about. Three months later I noticed that the spring thaw had begun, that the trees were turning green again, and that I could very well emerge not only from my room but also from my book. The novel was finished. I didn't work on it again until two years later, when I added a chapter and typed it. It was published in Lima in 1960, and it won the national novel prize that year.

I mention these circumstances to emphasize that this novel sprang from me spontaneously, without any outline or artistic and ideological assumptions, at least none that I was aware of. All that I can say about it is based on the result—that is, on the text itself.

For one thing, it is my only novel to take place in a rural setting, when I had always preached the need to write about Lima and to found an urban narrative tradition, practically nonexistent in Peru. I had set the example myself, when in 1955 I published my book of stories *Los gallinazos sin plumas.* The two novels I wrote after *Chronicle of San Gabriel—Los geniecillos dominicales* (1964) and *Cambio de guardia* (1976)—are also set in Lima.

Though *Chronicle of San Gabriel* takes place in the highlands, it isn't a novel of Indian life, a circumstance that differentiates it from the great Andean frescoes of Ciro Alegría and José María Arguedas. Its particularity is that it is a Lima native's view of the highlands. The indigenous peasant appears in it only sporadically, agricultural issues aren't dealt with explicitly, local color and folklore are absent, as well as all the political and social baggage characteristic of the indigenist novel. *Chronicle of San Gabriel* merely portrays the life of the landowners or the masters of an Andean hacienda and the ambiguous, tense, and often hidden relations troubling this microcosm.

Even so, some critics have found in this novel a range of meanings that I mention at random: a testament to the decay of large landed estates in the Peruvian highlands, a novel of formation or apprenticeship (the passage from adolescence to adulthood), a story of young love in a rustic setting, a simple novel of provincial manners, the novelized description of a clinical case of hysteria (Leticia), a cryptic work where the author has withheld information so that the reader can discover for himself a second work. These interpretations are interesting, and some are more defensible than others. As the author, I merely mention them, without taking sides.

Julio Ramón Ribeyro
Paris, March 1983

Table of Contents

THE TRIP

Cities, like people or houses, have a particular smell, often a stench. As I walked the straight Trujillo streets, I felt enveloped in a secret miasma emanating from somewhere or other, from porticos maybe, from condemned basements, or from the sewers. An unfamiliar smell reminded me at every step of my status as an outsider, son of a distant land. I was walking under the hot sun and the Moorish balconies, fanning myself, remembering how years earlier in Lima I had also noticed the smell of the city when I went downtown. Lima, old women used to say, smelled of clothes that had been packed away. For me it always smelled of baptisteries, pious women in shawls, big-bellied and dusty sacristans. But Trujillo smelled of something else. It was a yellow smell; in any case, a smell that had to do with egg yolks, vanilla ice cream, or the amber sun that penetrated everything.

The day before, at six in the morning, we had left Lima in a red bus. The trip was decided by my aunt and uncle, whose house I had been living in since my father's death. I never found out for sure why they decided to send me away from a place where I was beginning to feel comfortable. I suspected a plot by Aunt Herminia, who hated me because I spent all day doing nothing. My favorite pastime was to lean up against all the walls, flop into armchairs, and think about absurd things such as what Aunt Herminia's face would look like if she lost some of her hair. Or I would go up to the roof and busy myself chasing the rooftop cats around and spying on the neighbors. Since I had just finished school, I thought I had earned once and for all the right to spend time in idleness.

Maybe they thought my behavior would have a bad influence on my cousins, though really my truck with them was limited to an occasional punch. The fact is, Herminia's husband Felipe entertained me for several days talking about the hacienda he managed, about its pure air, the milk you could drink standing right next to the cow it came from. Since his words left me unmoved, he resolved to exercise his rights as my guardian, and one day he announced our trip.

So one summer morning Felipe and I left. The first day of the trip was memorably boring. I hadn't realized that my country's coast was a desert. Until then, I had known only the Lima valley, with its orchards and gardens. Through the window, I saw blowing sands, tan dunes taking shape and becoming lost to sight toward the east in depressing open terrain that called to mind an abandoned planet. Every hundred kilometers we crossed a river on whose banks sprouted weeds and shacks. Born on the plain in one way or another were parasite towns that lived off the highway the way you can live off a stream. The bus went by without conceding them the least importance, and on the shoulder of the main street, of the only street, you barely had the time to take in a hand moving in a sign that looked more like the desperate gesture of a man drowning than a greeting

In Trujillo we stayed at an old three-story hotel whose facade bore a sign depicting a five-pointed star. I was horrified by the high-ceilinged, papered, and crude rooms, and I did nothing but wander the streets in pursuit of the smell of the city. Felipe spent his days running around on strange errands. I saw him only at night; when he came back he would make noise and wake me up. I would open an eye and observe the mechanical gestures of a nighttime adventurer: he looked at himself in the mirror, fiddled with his mustache, stretched, and, whistling happily, got into bed. The last day of our stay in Trujillo I noticed he was more restless than usual. He paced back and forth between the bed and the balcony, lighting one cigarette with the butt of the other. At last he turned toward me and told me to leave the hotel right away and not to come back until after dinner. To make his order carry more weight, he gave me ten *soles*.

As I went down the stairs I noticed a woman on the sidewalk staring at the upper windows of the building. At the corner I turned around: the woman was crossing the street and going into the hotel.

That night, when I came back, I found a note from Felipe saying that we were going to leave for Santiago de Chuco at dawn. Close to midnight, I heard him come in. He was sunburned and had sand all over his clothes. When he noticed I was awake, he looked me over at length with shining eyes.

"A piece of advice," he whispered. "Don't ever believe in the purity of women. You know, there's no such thing as a pure woman, just a badly seduced one. All of them, listen up, all of them are equally corrupt at heart."

At four in the morning, my eyelids still swollen with sleep, I found myself in the cab of a truck heading for the Andes. We were packed in with a crowd of Indians returning to their lands with all their belongings: bundles of clothes, hens in sacks, handfuls of pungent herbs. Since Felipe didn't have anybody to talk to and since there was no greater torment for him than to have to be quiet, he made me his confidant and told me for a long time about his adventures on the road. When he was fourteen he had run away to the United States, where he spent his youth doing all kinds of jobs. That rough experience had carved on his features a trace of tenacity, resolve, and untamable strength that cowed men and subjugated women. I admired him profoundly and saw in him an example worth imitating.

At noon the storm began. Mud and rocks fell from the slopes. The overloaded truck could barely make it up the mountains. My face at the window, I watched the abysses going by. The driver, lulled by the sound of the engine, kept nodding off, so Felipe sat next to him and kept him awake with jokes and taps on the shoulder. Only at dusk did we make out the tiled roofs of the town. When I got out of the truck in front of the hotel I fainted. Later I opened my eyes to a strange, dirty room with newspaper on the walls. Felipe was at a table talking with a stranger and drinking at brief intervals from a bottle of pisco. The rain was drumming furiously on the windowpanes.

For several reasons we were held up a few days in Santiago. Our money had run out, it was raining, and the pack animals hadn't arrived. Felipe didn't lose himself in the streets this time; instead, he spent hours on the balcony observing the bad weather or stretched out in bed letting his beard grow. I kept myself distracted by putting an eye to a hole in the floor and spying on the hotel bar, where certain phenomena were taking place, exciting to someone as bored as I was, such as the pool games that always ended when the police chief, drunk by then, climbed up onto the felt and set about kicking the ivory balls.

One morning, Felipe, who was pacing the balcony, let out a shout: "Here they are!"

When I looked out I saw two huge dappled horses and a mule that the muleteer was holding by the bridle. Even though I had never ridden a horse, I had no choice this time, because just then facing that danger was better than staying in a fly-infested city, where you ate so badly in a market without tablecloths among coarse people who drank and belched. Two times in a row the horse made me kiss the still-damp Santiago ground. In the end I managed to stay in the saddle, gain some confidence, and gallop off to the head of the group.

At first we went down a wide, steep-walled ravine, taking a red-dirt path between two earthen walls. Prickly pear and agave kept us company until halfway down the slope. Then we saw roadside inns in the shade of the first eucalyptus trees. Farther down, close to the stream, the grain fields. Pure, dense air entered my mouth like a tonic and gave me the illusion of strength. At every step I felt myself arrested by the violence of the mountains, my sickly and pale city life gone forever.

After crossing the stream, we started up the opposite slope. The horses were breathing hard and stopped to drink from the springs. The air was getting thin. Everything calling to mind the presence of human beings was left farther and farther below. Even the path disappeared into a multitude of tracks hard to tell apart from gullies or the trails of some mountain animal. At last, when the vegetation disappeared and the breezes, which met no obstacles, were getting cold, we made it over the pass and in front of us there was nothing but a green plateau whose borders were lost in the distance. It was the Algallama pampa.

The engineer Gonzales, who came with us from Santiago, stopped his horse and said goodbye, taking the path to Cachicadán. Felipe watched him ride off and then calmly took a revolver out of his jacket and examined the barrel.

"You've got to be armed when you cross these pampas," he said when he noticed my astonishment. "Last year two ranchers were attacked. When you run into a horseman, stop on the right and don't start up again until he's out of sight."

Then he took a swallow of pisco, spurred his horse, and set off across the pampas.

It started raining in the middle of the afternoon. That immense plateau dotted with puddles, bristling with strange flattened cacti that looked like the excrement of some mythological beast, lowered my spirits and suddenly made me feel the fatigue of the journey. Only when we galloped our horses did I get excited, as if all at once I had been changed into another person or years had gone by since I left Lima. Felipe kept himself entertained by singing picaresque *huaynos* that the wind tore from his lips and carried away in confusion.

When we had crossed the pampas, we spotted the settlement of Angasmarca, born in the lee of a pyramidal rock. We dismounted at the local inn to wait for the rain to let up. Felipe ordered two steaks, got up from the table, and left. I saw him cross the street and disappear through a gate. Then he came back with a little boy hanging on his riding trousers. He caressed him and left him in the arms of a woman whose torso appeared between a pair of shutters. Then he came back to the inn, sat down on the bench, and with a huge appetite began eating his steak.

"Know who that is?" he asked me as he was chewing. "My son!" he added, bursting into happy laughter.

After coffee, we started out again, even though the weather was still bad. The paths had become ditches that the animals walked through with water up to their stirrups. We went up another ravine. A heavy shower blinded us. Felipe was no longer in a good mood, and he was riding pensively, his chin sunk into his chest. It was then that I had a strange feeling: that I was traveling a familiar path. The countryside had a secret language for me. I couldn't foresee the contours of the terrain or what was around a bend in the path, but once I saw them I took them in with recognition and was perturbed as if by a chance meeting with an old acquaintance. Felipe stopped suddenly at an inn.

"Dismount," he ordered.

An old Indian woman came out to greet us; she embraced Felipe with gaiety and offered us chicha. Felipe emptied his jug and had me go into an inner room that looked like a room for travelers. I was wondering if we were already at the hacienda. After looking through the window, Felipe came back quickly.

"This is where my father used to stay when he was police chief," he said, gazing at the cot. "Somebody—we never found out who—put his hand through the window and killed him with a bullet to the back."

That may have been some old family secret. But even though the story was an old one, it bothered me, as if it had to do with a recent calamity. We kept on under the omen of death. It was no longer raining, but we were riding through mud. Felipe was talking about his father, whom he always used to see cleaning his weapons to go out and fight mounted insurgents. Then he started telling me how I had to behave at San Gabriel.

"You've got to charm them," he was saying. "You don't get someone from Lima dropping in around here very often. You have to dance at the parties and entertain your cousins."

I was hardly listening to him. I was thinking about my grandfather found dead at dawn in that inn, his body cold and blue on his red sheet.

It was getting toward evening when Felipe abruptly reined in his horse.

"We made it," he said, pointing ahead. At the far end of a hollow you could see a mass of eucalyptus trees, a big white house with red roof tiles, and a red-earth path that ran out to our feet.

Halfway there we met them. Felipe dismounted and hugged them one after the other. But they remained uneasy, looking at me.

"Get down and greet your cousins," ordered Felipe. "They're your Uncle Leonardo's children. He's the owner of San Gabriel."

I struggled to dismount, to the point that I just about got myself dragged away by my horse. My cousins laughed. My stiffness must have been conspicuously ridiculous.

"Give them a hug," Felipe went on.

Mumbling some words of greeting, I embraced them. When I studied them more closely I noticed that the three looked quite different. The oldest one had fine but healthy features; the middle one was languid, transparent, and had dark circles under his eyes; the youngest, coppery and slant-eyed, had Indian blood.

"Where's Leticia?" I asked finally.

"I'm Leticia," said the oldest of the kids, taking off her hat. A lock of black hair fell over her forehead. I was surprised, and I couldn't help examining her body, which, under her men's clothes, looked like that of a fifteen-year-old boy.

"You're not going to give your cousin a kiss?" observed Felipe.

I froze. Never in my life had I kissed a woman, and all displays of affection bothered me. She was the one to move her head toward mine and brush my cheek with her lips.

"A mountain girl sets the example for you," said Felipe, but I had no answer. I was confused, annoyed, and my cousin must have noticed because she went serious all at once and, turning her back to us, took off running toward the house, chased by her dogs.

INCIDENTS

*I*n San Gabriel there was too much space for the smallness of my urban reflexes. I, who had spent most of my life in the three rooms of a *quinta*, seeing no face other than my mother's and no vegetation other than that on the dining-room wallpaper, felt immersed in a solvent atmosphere. Nothing, unless it was the horizon itself, limited my movements. In San Gabriel I lived spread out, strangely confused by the size of the land. Every evening, when I came back from exploring, I had to make an effort to reconstruct myself around my consciousness, but even so I couldn't prevent many of my footfalls, my finds, from remaining out there, lost in the country, without having been salvaged by my memory.

Besides, the presence of so many outsiders gave me the illusion of seeing myself multiplied by just as many mirrors. My Uncle Leonardo had turned the hacienda into a public inn and rural life into a perpetual fair. There wasn't a traveling rancher, engineer, salesman, or priest who wasn't retained by force and obliged to accept hospitality where wine served as the host and parties as the pillow. Every day a dozen hens, a lamb, a hog, or a deer was slaughtered. For me, contact with each new inhabitant meant not only the discovery of a new person but also the undertaking of transactions with a new part of myself. Everything led to variety. In that tumult, I tried to find both the places and the people I might have some affinity for.

Walking out of the orchard a few days after my arrival, I heard the sound of a musical instrument coming from a room close to the study. Since the door was ajar, I put my head in and saw a man bent over his mandolin, a score on the music stand. One of those unkempt beards grown almost for something to do, like the beards of the shipwrecked, covered his face.

The shadow I cast made him look around; the expression of child-ish terror in his blue eyes struck me as odd. He stood there a second watching me, his fingers motionless on the strings, until at last he seemed to recognize me. His mouth formed into a huge smile that had no rela-tion at all to the rest of his face, as if the different elements of his physi-ognomy were independent and could express contradictory feelings at the same time.

"You're Lucho, right? Come on in! I knew you were going to come."

As soon as I went in he started firing off questions that he didn't give me time to answer and then he told me he hadn't been down to Trujillo for twenty years and had been to Lima only once, as a child, when his mother was alive. Afterward, he took me around the room and showed me his things. The walls were covered with engravings. There were pictures of horses and soldiers and photos of a very young woman in all kinds of poses and outfits.

"That's my mother," he said, and after going quiet for a moment he explained he didn't let anyone in that room but would make an exception for me since I came from Lima, and what's more, would be his friend. As he spoke, he paced the room, adjusting with automatic movements the old hat he wore pulled down to his ears. He constantly avoided eye contact and his look tended to fix on some stationary and inanimate object around us.

"We have a lot to talk about," he repeated insistently. "There are lots of things you need to know. For you, we must be a little savage still. San Gabriel isn't a house, the way you think it is; it's not a town, either. It's a jungle."

As I reached over to his mandolin, he grabbed it quickly and stowed it in its case, but then, changing his mind, he took it out, and approaching the window, looking at the eucalyptus trees on the other side of the path, he began to play a doleful melody, one of those sad tangos that we've all heard maids singing in our childhood. While he played he kept time with his foot, and his body grew excited or relaxed to the rhythm of the music. I was unable to recover from my astonishment at finding myself, all at once, within the orbit of this character that nobody in San Gabriel had talked to me about.

That was when a third person entered the room. It was Leticia. She was surprised to see me.

"Plucking that mandolin again? Go check on the milking! You've got to be there so they don't steal the milk on us."

The mandolin man put down his instrument, tightened his belt, and left the room mumbling excuses.

Leticia stood there looking at me. It was obvious that my presence in that room displeased her. Then, with a slight gesture of annoyance, she surveyed the surrounding objects.

"What a mess in here," she said. "Ought to set it all on fire! Let's go eat breakfast. It's almost ready."

At ten in the morning the big breakfast was served. This was a custom established by my Uncle Leonardo to cater to the schedules of the different guests and to continue the highland tradition of communal meals. At seven the first breakfast was served, but only those who woke at dawn went, so it was a sad and boring breakfast. At ten, on the other hand, everybody was up, in a good mood, ready for a joke and an outing. My Aunt Ema, in addition to being a late sleeper, couldn't swallow a bite without a crowd around her, and it was also on account of this whim that the big breakfast in San Gabriel had taken on the majesty of a rite.

My Aunt Ema was short and mischievous, prone to guffawing at the slightest provocation. She sat at the head of the table in a special chair higher than the others, her small figure raised above that of the other diners. From there she directed the conversation, telling jokes, making ironic comments from one end of the table to the other, mocking everyone, including her husband. In the hacienda—which she always walked around in a bathrobe and high heels—she was something like a little empress, and the servants feared her capricious mood changes. But she seemed to be a good woman, because she put up with Uncle Leonardo's wildness. Ollanta, for example, was a son Leonardo had smuggled in; even so, Ema raised him together with her other children.

That morning there was talk of Lola's coming, and a luxuriant atmosphere prevailed in the hacienda. Everybody found this unexpected visit odd. Lola was another one of Leonardo's children, illegitimate like Ollanta, but with the difference that her mother wasn't a nameless Indian woman raped on a night of drinking but a rich landowner from a neighboring province on whom Leonardo had had to spend both mental energy and money. So Ema and Leticia were somewhat jealous and couldn't hide the annoyance caused by her imminent arrival.

"Maybe she's going to get married," said Ema, "and she's coming to ask for consent."

Felipe started.

"What? Is she already grown?"

"She's already twenty-one," answered Leonardo. "I haven't seen her for four years, but I imagine she must be a complete woman."

"And is she as pretty as Leticia?" asked Tuset, a textile salesman who was staying at the hacienda. "If that's the case we won't know which one to choose."

Leticia accepted this compliment without pleasure, and soon after she found a way to move her place setting to the other end of the table. For his part, Felipe had gone somber, and between sips of coffee he took drags on his morning cigarette. Meanwhile, the accountant's wife, a skinny and colorless woman everybody called the gringa, broke into a rant against people from Marañon when she found out Lola was from there.

"In general, Marañon women are bandits!" she screeched. "I knew two who poisoned their husbands. Besides, they're ugly, fat, and sun-burned."

The rest of her speech, whose viciousness seemed out of place to me, got lost in the general hubbub. There was talk then of a hunting party that would go out that afternoon to the lake with the ducks. Half-way through breakfast, the mandolin man came into the dining room and, without greeting anyone or looking up from his plate, ate with an appetite that staggered me.

We set out after lunch. Except for Ema and the gringa, everybody from the hacienda was going. The men went with their shotguns in ban-doleers, game bags on their backs. The mandolin man carried only a slingshot, as if he were lowered to the status of a child. From the start, he caught up with me and talked to me nonstop. Every ten steps he stopped to show me a view, a tree, since he knew the secrets of the path and seemed even to be friends with every pebble on the way.

"My name is Jacinto," he was saying. "But the half-breeds call me the *pishtaco*. I'll show you my mineral collection one day. Every time I go out for a walk I find a new rock."

I wasn't paying much attention to him. I couldn't explain it to myself, but something about him perturbed me. Tuset and Leticia were walking in front of us. My cousin was alternately approaching and flee-ing her suitor, giving him her hand at one moment and walloping him with a branch from an orange tree at another. Ollanta and Alfredo, prac-ticing their aim on birds, walked on top of the earthen walls beside us. My Uncle Leonardo, surrounded by his guests, the main body of the party, was walking farther ahead. Their loud laughter reached us. A wide milk can full of chicha was being carried by a servant and they were passing it from hand to hand. Daniel, the hacienda accountant, was bring-ing up the rear, his eyes wandering over the rocks on the path. From time to time he turned his head to look back at the roof of the hacienda. His squeamish and embittered look intrigued me.

"That Daniel does everything," Jacinto told me. "Among other things, he recruits laborers for the harvest and he charges so much per head. Besides that, he beats his wife."

"And why does he beat her?"

"How do I know? Here the big fish eats the little fish. The weak have no right to live."

When we got to the lake the men drank a last toast, looked over the bolts of their shotguns, and, led by Leonardo, headed into the brush on the lakeshore. I tried to follow them, but their cautious movements and long waits bored me. When I went back I saw Leticia trying to pull Jacinto's slingshot out of his hands.

"Give it to me!" she was saying. "You made the fork from a tree on my hacienda!"

Jacinto resisted, so she picked up a dirt clod and threw it at him without aiming.

"Stupid!" she shouted, withdrawing angrily to a clearing where Tuset was waiting for her. When she saw me, she took his arm and said to him:

"Let's go, dear. Help me find a fork."

The two of them disappeared. I stood next to Jacinto, who was playing quietly with the elastic bands of his slingshot. Lying down on the grass, I let myself fall into a stupor broken only by occasional gunshots. In the end, I fell asleep.

When I woke up, Leonardo and his bunch were laughing out loud, joking about the failure of the hunt. All together, they had managed to bag only two ducks and three doves. Daniel, who had brought a carbine, had amused himself target-shooting out in the open.

Something strange happened just before we started back. As Daniel was loading his carbine, it went off. The bullet brushed Felipe's shoulder and went into a tree.

SUNDAY

*T*he next day was Sunday. That day wasn't much different from the others, except for the visit from the Mollepata priest, who came on his little trotting mule to say mass. I didn't get that Lima Sunday feeling, because Sundays in Lima the sky took on a holiday color, the afternoon went by slowly, and the ice cream you bought from the cart wheeled by a man with a cornet managed to give the empty hours a chocolate flavor. The only one who seemed subject to Sunday fervor was Jacinto. That morning he was the first to stroll proudly under the arcades, clean-shaven, with a new hat on, a green three-piece suit, a tie, and three rings on his solid peasant hand.

The little priest arrived late. He was a lean mestizo, a great talker who wore a black coat over his cassock to keep the dust off. My cousin Alfredo put on an altar boy's suit and helped during mass, which was said at a prodigious speed. All the residents and servants of San Gabriel were at the chapel except Felipe, who couldn't stand the sight of a cassock.

"Priests are like crows," he would say. "When you see them wandering around a place, it's because someone's dead nearby."

I sat in the chapel next to Leticia that morning. Her lack of respect for the service surprised me from the start. She whiled away the time punching Ollanta, and when I looked at her reprovingly, she merely stuck her tongue out at me. But a little later she had calmed down, and I noticed she was curiously observing my spiritual absorption in my prayer book. In fact, my zeal was feigned and easily misinterpreted, because all I was doing was looking at the drawings in my missal or reading those strange prayers, written surely by some Jesuit, where, at times, piety seemed to get mixed up with lust.

"You're going to be a priest," whispered Leticia, turning her face toward me.

As I looked at her close up, I was astonished to discover that her pupils were of such unusual opacity that the light from the big windows lit them up without penetrating them.

After lunch, Leticia, who, unlike herself, had remained quiet, suggested an outing to the hill.

"Who wants to go with me?" she asked, looking around the table.

Tuset's hand went up right away. Unenthusiastically, Leticia acknowledged his loyalty, but then she added that they couldn't go alone, that someone else would have to go with them. Automatically, I raised my hand.

"Bravo!" exclaimed Leticia. "We'll rest at the shelter and then climb to the cross."

Tuset and I looked at each other for a moment; he held my gaze somewhat provocatively. Alfredo said he'd go on the walk, too, and after coffee the four of us got stirring. On the patio, a case of beer beside them, the guests stayed behind playing quoits.

I soon regretted my boldness. The "hill," as, in substitution of a descriptive word for a proper name, one of the highest peaks in the valley was called, was some distance away. We had to go down to a creek on a narrow, stony path enclosed by two big walls through whose cracks we could see open country. Leticia was running ahead, nimbly avoiding all the obstacles. Tuset, right on her heels, struggled to emulate her. I was at the rear, forgotten, stumbling on the rocks.

Halfway, Alfredo joined me. His long taciturn eyelashes, his predilection for solitude, had caused me to sympathize with him. I tried to win his confidence with stories and cajolery, but he stayed quiet. Only when I talked about Lima did he listen with any interest, and he interrupted me to ask how much money it would take to rent a house next to the ocean.

"I've never been to the ocean," he said. "In Trujillo I saw it once from a long way off. But I'd like to know how to swim and go way far out, so far nobody can see me and they all think I've gone to the bottom with the people who've drowned."

After that confession he went quiet. My attention was on the silhouettes of Tuset and Leticia, who were disappearing frequently around bends in the trail. My cousin's boldness annoyed me. From my Aunt Ema she had inherited an impertinent tone of voice, the authority of a little spoiled princess I couldn't stand anymore. But I couldn't help admiring her wildcat agility and her bravery. That's why I decided to copy her, and when I got to the creek, tired though I was, I suggested a race to see who could get to the cross first. My suggestion was taken up with delight, and soon the race began.

Only the fanaticism you have when you are fifteen let me put into that adventure the energy customarily expended on the important matters of life. I flung myself uphill wildly, not caring about the cacti or the rocks that were tearing holes in my clothes and skinning my hands. Forging a path where there was none, practically biting the ground, I made a breach of sweat and dust, and when I looked back a few minutes later I saw my competitors were coming leisurely up the wide slope, as if they had given up the fight.

They caught up with me a little later. Tuset told me sarcastically that I was a champion. Leticia, for her part, seemed to have forgotten the race already and was distractedly picking Spanish broom and making a bouquet of it.

"For you," she said, giving it to Tuset.

Turning my back on them, I went up to the cross. I don't know why I was hurt, and only the view from the peak could make me feel somewhat better. Hanging eucalyptus groves, lost hamlets, red paths, mountain ranges crowned by snow, and toward the east, a dark plain stretching off into the distance. It had to be the mountains, the jungle, the Marañon valley. Alfredo, who had caught up with me, was looking in the other direction. He didn't need to tell me—I realized he was trying to spot the ocean.

After I carved my name into the cross, a ritual undertaken by all outsiders, we headed down. Halfway down the hill, it started raining. Since there was an empty thatched hut, we took shelter in it. Leticia was quiet, and instead of resting her gaze on something she let it wander.

"I feel like sleeping," she said, lying down on the floor of the hut.

There was a pleasant half-light. Tuset sat down at her head and stayed there contemplating her. At times he looked at Alfredo, at me, as if he were regretting our presence. His hand, after a long, apparently absent-minded series of movements, managed to touch Leticia's. I didn't want to look and I turned my head. When I looked at them again, I saw that Tuset had withdrawn his hand. On the back of it he had a huge scratch. Leticia, a smile on her face, was pretending to doze.

At dusk we made it to San Gabriel, soaked, dirty, and starving. The four of us were in a bad mood and on the way back we had barely spoken. When I went into my room I decided to lie down and forget about dinner. I was about to get undressed when Felipe spoke to me. We shared the same bedroom, separated only by a wooden partition. When I went into his side, I saw him lying in bed. On his bedside table there was a bottle of brandy.

"What have you been getting yourself into?" he asked me. "You're all dirty. Go change and get into something elegant. Don Evaristo is here. He's the richest man around, an interesting fellow."

It seemed to me that he was a little drunk. His gestures were natural, but his slanted eyes had taken refuge so far back behind his cheekbones that they had become shining slots. Just as he was pouring a glass to give me a taste, a shadow fell across the room. It was Alfredo. When he saw Felipe, he stood motionless in the doorway, looking at him in terror.

"What are you doing here?" shouted Felipe, making as if to throw the contents of the glass at him.

Alfredo ran off.

"I don't know what's with that kid!" he continued. "He hates me; he spies on me. Or maybe he came just to talk with you. He'll end up crazy like his Uncle Jacinto!"

"Jacinto isn't crazy!" I protested.

"Everybody here is more or less crazy. Go get dressed. And rub your feet with snake oil because we're going to dance up a storm to-night."

Half an hour later I went into the living room. The guests were there, all together. Leonardo was wearing a gray country suit and beautiful calfskin boots. Ema and the gringa were dolled up, their lips enlarged by lipstick. Jacinto, with his hat on, was going from cluster to cluster, nodding unconsciously in approval of everything being said. Tuset was trying to pick up some music on the huge radio. Jisha, a young Indian who was acting as a butler, was opening bottles. Except for Daniel, who was reading a newspaper, everyone was tipsy, having been drinking since lunch. Ollanta and Alfredo came in later. It seemed to me someone was missing.

"Leticia's not feeling all that well," I heard Aunt Ema say. "She must have gotten too much exercise this afternoon."

Felipe was summoning me to introduce me to Don Evaristo when a woman entered the room. I didn't recognize her at first. I was so used to seeing Leticia in trousers that when I saw her in a clinging red dress and high heels, her hair hanging elegantly over the nape of her neck, I was confused. She paused by my side, stood up straight, and without a word went over to the group of the older people.

Felipe had followed her with his gaze. When I approached him I heard him saying to the rancher:

"She can get married now. Tuset won't have to wait too long."

There was a glass of beer within reach. Instinctively, I seized it and, with my eyes closed, drank it in one go.

Dinner took place with rather desperate intensity. Right away, Don Evaristo became conversation director. He was about sixty, white-haired already, but had hard and manly features and energetic gestures that suggested invincible power. He had complete mastery of the art of storytelling; while we were eating and drinking, he kept us entertained with regional, fantastic, or obscene stories featuring priests, prefects, governors, landowners, villagers. His loud voice filled the dining room, crashed into the walls, and when he burst out laughing the glassware shook. His wife was a pretty, languid, and quiet woman from Lima, so young she could have passed for his daughter, whom he dragged with him on all his trips as a kind of decoration, the same way you might wear a pin on your lapel. She looked a little lost in that noisy party and immediately exchanged a few glances of recognition with me. Children as we were of sea and dunes, our presence in that place was almost a mistake of nature.

At one point Don Evaristo became indignant, and in his indignation he attained a fascinating stature. His fists tore at the bread and pounded the table; meanwhile, words that could have flattened a man spewed forth from his mouth. He was complaining about the Indians of a village community, who had petitioned to expropriate part of his land. An engineer had already left Lima to visit the disputed area and report on whether the expropriation should proceed.

"Would it by chance be Engineer Gonzales?" asked Felipe. "We ran into him in Santiago de Chuco. He stayed a few days in Cachicadán, but he should be around here pretty soon."

"I hope he's a reasonable fellow," answered Don Evaristo.

That sentence, so simple, must have had another meaning, because Leonardo and Felipe burst out laughing.

As dessert time grew nearer, the ruckus got louder and louder. Everybody was talking at the same time. All the diners, including Alfredo and Ollanta, were greedily drinking white wine. I emulated them and was immediately tempted to provoke Tuset. The last few days the sight of him had become intolerable to me. Taking advantage of a momentary calm, I dared to raise my voice so everybody could hear me:

"I raced Tuset to the top of the hill this afternoon and left him in the dust. Tuset's from the highlands and I've only been here a week."

The observation was childish. But I noticed that Tuset went red. Everybody laughed, even Don Evaristo, and the grown-ups, delighted, congratulated me. Tuset's reply was lost in the uproar, but from the look in his eyes I gathered it had been offensive. Emboldened by my success, I looked at Leticia and added:

"I beat her, too."

Leticia went serious, grew pale, and shot me a brief, terribly cunning glare that hurt me like a blow. But by then we were all getting up to go to the drawing room, where the dance was awaiting us. Getting up from the table, Jacinto fell on the floor, taking with him several plates. Leonardo ordered him to go lie down.

In the drawing room, apart from the radio, there was an old wind-up record player of the kind you don't see anymore. Leticia was choosing the records and playing them without letting anyone interfere. When Ollanta made an approach, he was brutally rejected. That act of despotism troubled me, and I thought Leticia was really hateful.

The music was deplorable: pasodobles, old fox trots from the period between the wars, military marches; even so, everyone was dancing. Leticia was dancing with fascinating elegance, so much so that the men were quarreling to take her out on the floor. From a corner, I saw her pass from arm to arm, holding her head high, svelte on her high heels. Felipe, chewing on his cigar, was watching her too. After several dizzying turns with the woman from Lima, Daniel had flopped onto a sofa.

I kept looking at Leticia. I felt an acute need to humiliate her. Her happiness, which I didn't share, her easy triumph, caused me to bear her an incomprehensible grudge. Paying attention to no one, she continued twirling, her eyes half-closed, given over to the music with extreme sensuality. At one point she passed by me in Tuset's arms. He looked at me and couldn't help laughing.

"So look at the Lima boy. All dressed up, but he can't dance a step."

To prove him wrong, I asked the woman from Lima to dance, but after two songs, during which I behaved awkwardly, she abandoned me on a friendly pretext. Meanwhile, the dance was continuing with a force that seemed to portend a coming orgy. Leonardo and Don Evaristo were giving each other big hugs. Daniel, a bottle in his hand, was shouting out insults from his armchair. Even Tuset was about to fall over, and with his partner gone, he was dancing alone and stumbling on the furniture. The only one to keep his sanity was Felipe, who was taking turns dancing with Ema and the gringa.

Leticia had disappeared. I don't know why I suspected she must have been under the patio arcades. Filling a glass with beer, I got ready to go look for her, my intentions unclear even to myself. I thought maybe I could pretend to trip and spill the drink on her beautiful scarlet dress. When I went out, I saw her leaning on a column, indifferently watching the rain fall on the corral. I approached slowly until I was right behind her. When she sensed my presence, she turned around quickly and looked at me. The violent anger of her expression astounded me.

"What are you doing with that glass?" she asked.

I raised it to my lips.

"You're an idiot!" she went on. "You told everyone about the hill! Who are you to talk? Where are you from? Don't you know not to mess with me?"

Since I couldn't manage to answer, she took a step toward me.

"Next Sunday we'll run a race to the river, just you and me. Then we'll see who wins. And whoever comes in first…. Whoever comes in first gets to do whatever he wants to the other one. Bite him, maybe, in the ears, the nose, and the fingers."

As she said that she went quickly back to the drawing room and in the doorway she ran into the gringa, who was pulling on a drunken Daniel by the arm. After leading him a few steps she let him fall to the ground. His head hit with a bang and I thought I saw her kicking him. Scared, I hid behind a column. The gringa went into the drawing room and reappeared with Felipe.

"You better help me with him," she said, and between the two of them they dragged him across the rainy patio.

I headed for my bedroom bewildered, worn out by the long day. Felipe came back at dawn, when you could already distinguish a hint of blue through the window. As in the hotel in Trujillo, when he was coming back from one of his nocturnal outings, I heard him whistling joyfully as he got undressed.

THE MESSAGE

*F*rom then on life in San Gabriel began to reveal itself to me in a different light. What I took for wild celebrations and the love of disorder were signs of secret and renewed domestic tensions. Relationships between one person and another were governed by a thousand inconceivable details. At times, all it took was laughing with someone to fall out of somebody else's good graces. A gesture, a word, put the microcosm on the brink of revolution.

For one thing, Daniel and the gringa stayed away from the dining room for several days. From the drawing room, I saw them under the north-facing arcades, sitting in their wicker chairs, reading old magazines. Daniel had a bandage on his forehead and he was drinking beers that Jisha brought him by the dozen. When they took up the family routine again, they did so dressed elegantly, as if this change of clothing revealed a more profound determination: to change their attitudes toward the other residents. Daniel chose his words with care when he spoke, and the gringa, keeping her mouth shut, took care only to hide the bruises adorning her forearms. Those dark traces couldn't have been left by caresses.

For her part, Ema had become irritable. She banged the plates at the table, spared nobody her sarcasm, and devoured with her glares those who dared confront her. Even Leonardo seemed mistrustful, though he had other reasons. The newspapers were bringing him bad news: the war was about to end and the tungsten mines he managed were becoming less and less profitable.

I soon saw myself enveloped in a feast of peevishness. It stemmed from a conversation I overheard through the wall separating my room and the study. When I heard Leticia's name I put my ear to the wall (along with the words, strange sounds from the blacksmith's reached my ears, from the kitchens, from the stable, all sorts of sounds living enclosed in rock). Tuset and Leonardo were arguing delicately. Their dispute reached me in fragments, and I had to reconstruct them after my fashion.

"But how are you going to get married?" Leonardo asked clearly. "You're not even engaged yet!"

Tuset's answer was drowned out by other noises.

"Come back later," continued Leonardo. "We'll have to talk about it with Leticia."

That dialogue left me baffled. I wondered if Leticia was capable of agreeing to that negotiation. Everything suggested that she was aware of something; for as long as Tuset was around she kept wearing her party dress, treated everybody with cold politeness, and put on a languid and pensive look. Only when her suitor left did she start wearing trousers again and acting like a rowdy boy.

With the departures of Tuset and Don Evaristo, the atmosphere changed. The engineer Gonzales arrived soon after, which made passions become organized or feigned in terms of this new personality. The engineer tried to set off right away for Don Evaristo's lands, but Leonardo retained him, somewhat surprised by his guest's aversion to alcoholic beverages. Since it was a tradition that nobody spent the night in San Gabriel without getting drunk, Gonzales was attended to opulently, getting all kinds of bizarre potions in whose concoction Felipe, Ema, and Leonardo cooperated crazily, until one night he was seen crying and vomiting in the pastures. Having gone through that initiation, he was at the mercy of the road, but it was just then that he became stubborn about staying. Every morning he put off his departure.

"It's strange," he would say to Felipe. "But I'd be happy to stay here. If it weren't for that damn job! It's not superstition, just wariness. It's strange! I've never been so tempted to stay somewhere and say, 'Everything else can go to hell!'"

Even so, he left on a mare lent him by Leonardo. As soon as he was out of sight, we forgot all about him.

The last few days I had picked up the habit of waking up early to help with the milking. In the small barn I would drink the warm, sweet, and foamy yellow milk that went from udder to bucket. Then I would go see Jacinto, who hadn't shown himself much since Sunday and was spending most of his time playing his mandolin. In general, he tolerated my presence but didn't talk. Sometimes he put his instrument down and stood gazing out the window at the dove-filled woods; he could spend hours like that and nobody could wake him up. Except for those of his mother, all the pictures had disappeared from the walls.

That morning he was rather excited. When I went in he grabbed me by the arm and took me to his table.

"Look," he said, showing me some books. "They're electricity lessons. I got them from Trujillo. Engines are really interesting, but there's a lot I don't understand. Don't you have a dictionary?"

I recalled that in the room Leticia and Alfredo shared there was a trunk full of books. It wouldn't have surprised me to find a dictionary there. With that hope, I left. I had been in their room only a few times,

always in a group, when on account of one of those phenomena of movement, inexplicable in social life, the greater part of the family ended up
there to finish a conversation. The door was ajar, and just as I was about
to go in I heard Leticia talking to Alfredo.

"I don't want to!" she was saying passionately. "If that happens
I'll throw myself in the river."

"But Dad thinks of him as a son."

"I know, but he has nothing in common with us."

"Besides, people respect him in Santiago, and they're going to
make his father mayor."

Relieved, I realized they were talking about Tuset.

"That may be how it is, but I don't want to get married!"

"You're picky," continued Alfredo. "Besides, you're mean because
you don't love anybody."

"That's right. I don't love anyone."

"What if you married Lucho?"

Leticia let out a scream.

"Are you crazy?"

Just then I pushed open the door. Leticia was in her pajamas, sitting on her bed and painting her toenails with a very fine brush. She was
surprised to see me; her expression darkened.

"What do you want?" she asked. "Have you been spying?"

"Spying on what?" I replied as I entered the room. She went on
with her task, not bothering to cover herself with the bedclothes. Alfredo
turned toward the wall. "I came for a dictionary."

"I don't have a dictionary," answered Leticia without looking up.

"There might be one in the trunk."

Stepping over to the old hulk, I opened it and put my hands into a
pile of dust, papers, and lint. They were mostly old novels by unknown
authors, like almost all the books you see in libraries in the highlands,
collected as they are by farmers and old maids with no taste at all. But
the editions were luxurious, with illustrations in color and hard covers.
All at once I felt uneasy, and when I turned around I saw Alfredo approaching aggressively.

"Get out of there!" he shouted, pushing me away from the trunk.
"There's nothing in there!" he said, closing the cover and sitting down
on top of it before I could react. "It's not worth looking for anything in
there. You'll just get your hands dirty."

Leticia had finished painting her nails. Putting her feet together,
she inspected her work.

"So? Did you find anything?" she asked. "They're mostly boring old books. One of these days I'm going to burn them. They bother me."

"Everything bothers you. Do you even know how to read?"

Leticia looked up and threw the brush to the ground. She had gone red.

"I can teach you whenever you want. I can even read English!"

She pulled the bedclothes over herself at once. Her body was shaking under the covers. I had the impression she was crying. I was disconcerted, unable to move, not knowing what to do. Alfredo had gotten into bed again. On his lips there was a scab. I remembered that a few days earlier, when I was out walking with Gonzales, we had found Alfredo crying under a blackberry bush. Leticia raised her voice from underneath the blankets.

"Are you brave?"

"Yes," I answered resolutely.

"Then go to Ollanta's room and hit him. Hit him until he cries."

"What for?"

"Alfredo says that yesterday he was saying something bad about our mother."

"What did he say?"

"I don't know, but his mother's an Indian and he shouldn't be with us. Besides, he bullies Alfredo because he's stronger."

In other circumstances I wouldn't have obeyed her, but having offended Leticia, I committed myself to making it up to her. I ran out to the patio. Under the arcades Ollanta was playing with one of the hacienda dogs. I sneaked up behind him, and latching on to his neck I punched him hard in the head. Ollanta started wailing, but by then Felipe, who had seen it all, was approaching us angrily.

"What did you do that for?"

I didn't know what to say.

"I have a cure for bullies," he added, walking off to the blacksmith shop.

I took refuge in Jacinto's room. I told him I hadn't found the dictionary, but he wasn't paying any attention to me. He was cutting his lessons into long strips with a penknife and stacking them at his feet. I went out the gate and headed for the eucalyptus grove. I was worried about the reprisals Uncle Felipe might take. Once I heard him say he had put a lying servant in a well full of water until he lost consciousness. When it came to punishments, he had a fertile imagination. As I gathered dead leaves I tried to relax. When I got all I needed, I wrapped them in my pullover and went back with the idea of making a bonfire to drive off the evening mosquitoes.

It must have been time for the big lunch. On the patio I saw a lot of people standing around in an attitude of expectation. Intrigued, I headed over to find out what was happening when Felipe, pointing at me, shouted:

"There he is!"

Before I could get away he grabbed me by the neck, and twisting my arm he made me drop my load. The leaves scattered. Then he started dragging me, saying:

"My father made me fight against two, but with you I won't be so demanding."

I saw the Negro Reynaldo emerge from the smithy with two pairs of boxing gloves. The thought that I was going to be forced to fight that giant terrified me. Felipe must have guessed what I was thinking.

"I don't want to see you die just yet. You're going to fight Jisha. But listen up: with only one hand."

Jisha was getting his gloves put on just then. He was the household servant, a graceful Indian who was shorter than I was but much older. I hadn't exchanged a word with him other than to give him orders, and since he was used to obeying only his usual masters, my newcomer's authority struck him as inadmissible. On several occasions, he had ignored me. Hitting one hand into the other, he was looking at me with a smile all over his face.

Rebellion was pointless. Putting up no resistance, I let my left arm get tied behind my back. The spectators had formed a circle and they looked serious, as if, deep down, these preparations perturbed them. In a corner, Leticia and Alfredo were watching me in silence, holding hands. The only one who protested was the gringa.

"You should at least let him use both hands!"

"No fun that way," answered Felipe. "Bullies have to be punished. He hit Ollanta for no reason. If he'd just say why did it—but he's as stubborn as a mule."

I caught Leticia's eye, but in her expression I saw nothing other than utter indifference.

The fight must have lasted five minutes, but I had lost all notion of time, of the things around me, and with my one free hand I flailed wildly. Around me rose a constant uproar. At one point, my nose smashed, Jisha threw me against a wall and I thought I was dying. Blood stained my shirt. I kept struggling, must have been using my feet since several voices protested. Jisha's eyes pursued me relentlessly, and the sight of his lips, closed one moment and mockingly open the next, harried and fled me. Then I saw them split, spurting black blood. In the end, weariness took my breath away and I couldn't lift my arm. I had fallen to the ground unconscious, taking my opponent's blows like a bag getting shaken out.

Someone shouted "Enough!" and when I opened my eyes I saw Jacinto running toward my adversary. Felipe stepped into his path, but he couldn't stop a kick from knocking the servant flat on his face. Shouts broke out. Leonardo and the women intervened. When I broke the rope tying down my left arm, I fled to my room while Jacinto was led off to one side and a screaming Jisha to another.

As a sign of protest I stayed in my room all day. At times I was tempted to run to the pasture, saddle a horse, and head for Santiago. In the end, I fell asleep.

As evening drew near, a voice sounded by my side. I opened my eyes and saw Alfredo.

"Here's your food," he said, putting a plate wrapped in a napkin on the night table.

I tried to get up, but he stopped me.

"Don't move around. It's better if you rest until tomorrow. Leticia gave me something for you."

Putting his hand in his pocket, he took out a sheet of paper folded in four.

"See you tomorrow," he said, giving it to me and disappearing.

I hastened to unfold the sheet of paper. At first I thought it was blank, but then, in one of the corners, I saw a short sentence: "Remember, tomorrow's Sunday." The meaning was indecipherable to me at the time. I even thought she was just trying to prove to me she knew how to write. With the sheet of paper in my hands, I fell asleep again.

THE PUNISHMENT

*T*he next morning, I had just woken up when Felipe approached my bed.

"How's that nose doing? You were brave yesterday! Good. Congratulations. I didn't come to see you earlier so it wouldn't go to your head."

I didn't say anything, so he began pacing between the window and the door, talking all the while. Among other things, he was saying that women wouldn't leave him alone, that two of them had written from Trujillo, and that he was authorizing us to reply that he had drowned in the Marañón. Suddenly, he sat down on the bed and seized my wrist.

"You know something and you're going to tell what it is right now," he said, his eyes scrutinizing me intolerably. "I don't like people who keep secrets. You didn't hit Ollanta just because. You must have had some reason."

I didn't have any secrets and I wasn't interested in keeping any. The only thing I was afraid of was getting Leticia in trouble. Omitting any allusion to her, I replied:

"I hit him because he hit Alfredo."

"And why did he hit Alfredo?"

"He's always hitting him. At least that's what I heard. I don't like bullies, either."

Felipe let go of my wrist and smiled maliciously.

"It seems," he added, hesitating, "that Ollanta said something bad about Aunt Ema."

Felipe got up to look calmly out the window. After a while he left the room without a word.

I went over to the mirror and looked at my face. The swelling of my nose had gone down, but I had a purplish ring around my eye. At that moment I resolved to learn how to box so that one day I could get revenge on Jisha. The Negro Reynaldo would be happy to have a student.

When I went out to the patio, I ran into Felipe and Leonardo, who were walking under the arcades chatting.

"Engineer Gonzales is a good man," Felipe was saying. "But he's too young to confront a crafty fellow like Don Evaristo. The old man will offer him a low price, and he'll have to accept it because, in addition to other reasons, he's getting married. What an idiot! Getting married in the prime of his youth! I'd devote myself to collecting little provincial girls, as pretty as they are poor and so affectionate, too."

I left them. Felipe's jokes disheartened me more and more. I admired his generosity, his bravery, but I couldn't forgive the biting tone and the lack of respect he had for the feelings of others. In his mouth the words love, wife, home, religion—huge words for me—took on a sneering sound that made them ridiculous.

Wandering around the patio, I tried to find Leticia. In my pocket I had her message and I wanted her to help me decode it. I soon dared to go into her room, but it was empty. As I walked the dark passageway leading to the kitchen, I saw her coming out a side door. When she saw me she walked quickly toward me and went right by me without looking. Before I could open my mouth she had disappeared.

Nervous, troubled by a vague premonition, I went to talk with Jacinto. Even though that morning was Sunday, I found him unshaven, wearing his pajama tops. He was sitting at his desk going over his books on electricity. When he saw me he stared at my black eye. Only after a long silence did he ask what had happened to me. So much did his question surprise me that I stood there with my mouth hanging open. It seemed to me incomprehensible that in such a short time he could have forgotten what had happened.

"I hit myself on the window," I answered.

He looked at me suspiciously. Maybe he recalled something but didn't dare say it.

"I think you've been fighting someone," he began. "Wasn't it yesterday that you fought somebody? Maybe it was just a nightmare."

"It's the time of year for bad dreams," I answered.

"I have horrible dreams," he added, squeezing his temples. (His expression was of such bitterness that it left me astounded. I was reminded of the small, terrible masks my cousins carved out of saponite, a soft river rock.) "Why are people so awful?" he shouted, giving me a singularly lucid look. "Everybody does harm, nothing but harm…. War, revolutions, abuses. Can't we live in peace? People offend each other, get irritated, spend their lives persecuting each other, for fun, most of the time, without needing to, just so they don't get bored. Then they get old and die. The end! It's not worth it."

He went on speaking for a while. At first it seemed to me that he was rambling, but then I realized that his ideas were right and that his abnormality lay precisely in an excess of common sense. This discovery stupefied me, and I wondered if everybody else was completely crazy and he was the only sane one. Felipe's coarse passion for women or Leonardo's zeal to profit off tungsten seemed much more dangerous to me.

Jacinto had stood up.

"I'm not going to mass today," he said. "I'm ashamed of all those hypocrites hitting themselves on the breast, starting with the priest, who admits he's got a wife and child in Angasmarca when he gets drunk. Let's go see Marica. I haven't paid her a visit for a while."

I had occasionally heard an allusion to Marica, but such a vague one that I was never sure if people were talking about a real person. Before I could interrogate Jacinto, he had put on a pullover and left the room. I could barely keep up with him. We went down several corridors. The house at the hacienda was huge, a true walled fortress. After much opening and closing of doors we made it to a twilit room. Jacinto opened a high window and on a straw-matted chair I saw a strange creature made of skin and bones. It was an old woman whose age was impossible to tell.

"How are you, Marica? It's Jacinto. I'm coming to visit you. I opened the window to let in a little sun. It's a nice day."

On the old woman's face, framed by a shawl, a shifting of wrinkles took place. Her lips twitched into an expression of sweetness and she nodded several times to let him know she had recognized him. But her eyes, set deep under her red eyelids, were viscous and round, like peeled grapes.

"She's blind," Jacinto said to me, lowering his voice. "And deaf, too, I think. Nobody knows how old she is."

"Who is she?" I asked finally.

"Aunt Ema's grandmother. She's been closed up in here for years. Julia, the kitchen maid, is in charge of preparing her food and getting her up, but sometimes she forgets. Sad, isn't it? But what can be done with her? She can't walk and there aren't any wheelchairs here. If we take her out to the patio she might catch a cold. I sometimes think she should die. Did you get your chamomile tea?" he asked, turning toward her.

The old woman made no sign. Her head turned in my direction, she seemed to be somewhat curious, as if she had sensed the presence of an outsider.

"This is Lucho, my nephew," Jacinto went on. "He came from Lima to visit you. He's going to give you his hand."

Then I felt on my palm the touch of that cold claw. Instinctively, I let it go. It seemed to me that I had been touched by death. There was something in that old woman that no longer belonged to the order of the living, and I realized why people always talked about her as if about an ambiguous creature lying halfway between the world and the tomb.

Jacinto was talking to her again. He was telling her what he had been doing the last few days, his diversions, his minor problems. In the end he started talking to her about engines and telling her how a dynamo worked. The little old woman was nodding, but it was clear she didn't understand a word.

Little by little I withdrew toward the door. That spectacle pained me. It seemed to me that when Jacinto was talking he was addressing himself, or, with his mute interlocutor, satisfying his need to communicate. When I got to the door, I opened it and ran off.

It was only when I was on the patio, dazzled by that brilliant day calling to go out and enjoy it, that I understood the meaning of Leticia's message: it was referring to our race to the creek. That discovery excited me greatly, but at the same time it worried me. I still felt battered from the fight the day before; my muscles ached. There was no point asking Leticia for a postponement. There was no sign of her.

At lunch I managed to see her. The priest, as usual, started drinking beer and arguing with Felipe. I was hardly listening to that violent dialogue, spiced now and then with obscenities, about dogma. My attention was focused solely on Leticia, who was eating without looking up from her plate. In her hair was a piece of straw, so I guessed she had been in the grain loft. Only once did she make so bold as to look at me and when she did so it was with such resolve that I dropped my gaze. My Uncle Leonardo, for his part, was grave, talking quietly to Aunt Ema. At times he would look carefully at all the diners as if he were trying to identify someone. At the end of the meal he imposed silence by banging on the table and said he was going to talk about a very serious matter.

"A large sum of money has disappeared from my desk," he began. "Part of what I was setting aside to pay the miners. If anyone has a clue, let me know. In fact, it must have been stolen a few days ago, but it was only when I did the audit this morning that I noticed."

Angry silence followed those words. Everybody at the table looked at each other. Jisha, coming in with the coffee just then, stood motionless in the doorway. The only face where I saw something other than plain surprise was Daniel's: leaning back in his chair, he stared quietly at the ceiling. I remembered then the way he walked at the rear the day of the hunt, his continual looks back. What Leticia did next also surprised me: she stood up and rushed out of the dining room.

An hour later I was sitting under one of the arcades with my feet out on the patio and my eye on the gate leading to the pastures. I hadn't seen Leticia since the dining room, but if our bet was still on she would have to go through that gate, which was the only way to the river. The news of the robbery had lowered everybody's spirits, a change that didn't keep the usual abundant drinking from getting underway. Leonardo and Felipe were walking behind me, and it seemed strange to me to hear the latter discussing Ollanta and Alfredo in paternal terms.

"You shouldn't neglect their education," he was saying. "You should send them to school in Santiago as soon as possible."

Then Leticia came out of her room and walked toward the gate. When she had gone through it, I stood up and started following her. She had already made it to the path and was walking along absent-mindedly, picking up pebbles. When she heard my footsteps she paused and turned around. Even though the air was cool, she had two red blooms on her cheeks.

"Did you bring my piece of paper?" she asked, holding out her hand.

"I haven't left it for a second," I replied, grabbing her fingertips.

She withdrew them immediately.

"I'm not greeting you," she said, suddenly serious. "I'm asking you for my piece of paper."

I gave it to her and she crumpled it in her hand without reading it. Then she tore it into pieces that she threw to the wind. As she was doing so her expression flickered and went dark.

"Felipe is not a good person," she said. "He's an old bully. One of these nights, since you sleep next to him, you should hit him on the head with a stick, hard, until you beat a big hole open."

I had already noticed it, but it was then that I realized to what extent Leticia was prone to cruelty. The thought that I might lose the race and receive the agreed-upon punishment terrified me.

"I'm a little tired," I began. "My legs hurt. We should just go for a walk.

"Ah! So you're afraid! When I climbed the hill I was sick too, but even so...."

"What did you have?"

She went red.

"Nothing. I'd eaten too much."

"Let's go for a walk," I insisted.

"No walks. I don't like walking with other people. Look, we'll walk to that bend and when we get to the tree we start running. And remember the punishment!" she added, opening her lips slightly to show her small white teeth.

A little disturbed, I took off after her. As far as the bend we walked side by side, without speaking. When we got to the tree, Leticia shouted "Go!" and took off running like someone possessed. I was behind her and soon realized that with an effort I could catch up, but to give her the momentary illusion of victory I chose to hold back. But over the rough sections she increased her lead, since she avoided the puddles and rocks with devilish nimbleness. I was starting to get tired and I still couldn't see the slope of the hill the river ran around. Leticia kept getting farther ahead, her hair in the wind, not bothering to look back. I sped up just then and her lead started shrinking. The first riverbank vegetation appeared. Leticia was almost within reach of my hand, when coming around a curve, I tried to avoid an agave plant sticking out of a wall and fell face-forward to the ground. For a few seconds I remained immobilized by the pain, unable to get up. When I finally did, I saw I had a cut on my knee. Even so, I started running again. The path ahead of me was empty. Maybe Leticia had taken advantage of the occasion to jump over the wall and run through the pasture; at any rate, when I got to the river I saw her leaning over the bank, soaking her face in the current.

"I beat you!" she shouted, turning to splash water on me. "Now you can't say anything! I'll tell everybody tonight. I beat you!" And she began jumping around me and clapping with delight.

When she saw my battered look, she stopped. I rolled up my pants' leg to show her my cut and move her to pity.

"No excuses," she protested. "Later, you can do whatever you want, but for now you should remember our agreement."

"What agreement?" I asked, pretending not to know about it.

"The punishment."

When she said that she lost all her charm. In vain did I seek in her expression just then a sign that she was only kidding. I tried to escape as Leticia came after me, but I could barely manage to drag myself to a tree and lean against the trunk. Leticia was approaching slowly. She was pale and she was panting as if the fatigue of the race had come back.

When she put her hands on my shoulders, I closed my eyes, fearing myself lost, but then I felt something sweet all over. Her lips were on my cheek, but instead of hurting me they were seeking my mouth, finding it, and entering it like the flesh of a fruit asking to be devoured. I put out my arms and tried to hold her, but it was impossible. Letting go of me, she jumped over an adobe wall and disappeared into an alfalfa field.

THE AGRONOMIST'S RETURN

*T*he next few days I was in a constant daze and barely noticed what was happening around me. I spent hours and hours in my room, then rushed off to the pastures to exhaust myself on absurd walks. I had returned to the riverbank several times, to that tree in whose shade I had experienced such strange magic. The solitary country only increased my irritation.

Leticia was always avoiding me. When we were in a group, she behaved with perfect naturalness, holding my gaze with cynicism, and even speaking to me with a confusing combination of familiarity and insolence. But as soon as the possibility of a conversation between just us arose, she got extremely nervous and found a way to disappear.

My bewitchment must have stimulated Alfredo's curiosity, because he came to see me in my room several times. He would wander around my stuff then, picking up my books, examining my clothes. I had the impression that his admiration for me was growing. He often asked me to tell him a story or read him a book, a favor I did him for something to do, my mind being occupied elsewhere. During one of those readings he suddenly broke into tears. He was curled up in the bed and shaking like a malaria victim. When I asked him what was wrong, he told me his father was planning to send him to school in Santiago soon.

"I don't want to go to Santiago," he complained. "And even less with Ollanta. He'll hit me all the time and end up killing me. It's all Uncle Felipe's fault. He gave my father the idea ."

"But it's past time for you to start studying."

"Yes, but I want to go to Mollepata; it's only half an hour away on horseback. But if I go to Santiago I'll have to spend nine months at school sleeping at Mabila's house. What's happening is that they want me out of here, me and Ollanta both; they want to keep us a long, long way away."

"Why?"

"Why? I don't know! Felipe, who's so macho, is afraid of me. Ask him! But if they want to send me away they don't have to send me to Santiago. I'll go myself somewhere else. We've already thought about it."

Those confessions made me think. I suspected something was happening, something out of sight, but I had too few clues to come up with a solid conjecture. I observed my Uncle Felipe, whose behavior seemed singularly equivocal. The frankness, the spontaneity of his actions, seemed guided by the subtlest calculation. His gestures, his words, were never gratuitous and they always had a hidden meaning that could be understood only by those who possessed the key.

One night I thought that key would be revealed to me when, already late, after dinner, the two of us alone in the bedroom, he asked me to do him a favor.

"Go to the gringa's room," he told me, "and give her a message."

I waited anxiously for the contents of that message.

"Tell her it's going to rain tonight and to be careful of leaks."

That sentence was clear, but at the same time it had a series of meanings that made it confusing. What disconcerted me most was that a violent storm actually broke that night and kept me awake until late. Before midnight, there was a furious knocking on the front gate, followed by curses and shouts. I heard the dogs go by barking under the arcades, then the night watchman heading to see what was happening. When the gate was opened, the uproar grew louder. Felipe, who was sleeping peacefully, woke with a start. Soon after, Leonardo, who was carrying a flashlight, and Ema, wearing a robe, came into the room.

"It's Daniel coming back drunk," said Leonardo. "He left for Angasmarca on a job, but it looks like he had to turn back because of the storm."

What most surprised me was the strange pallor of my Aunt Ema's face.

The only person to remain unmoved by all these incidents was Leticia. Her life was of a special order not easily penetrated by the passions of others. Maybe it was a kind of selfishness or a complete lack of artifice. She had been wearing glasses the last few days—probably with non-correcting lenses—and would spend hours reading a volume of *The Treasury of Youth*, the bustle around her not causing her to look up. All my attempts to approach her had been fruitless. Her most recent tactic was to pretend not to hear me.

Taking advantage of my sudden closeness with Alfredo, I tried to find out something about her. I bugged him with questions that he answered rather cagily. I found out through him that Leticia hadn't said a word about our excursion to the river. The thought of sharing a secret with her seemed to me a first triumph. Then I found out that when Alfredo told her I knew lots of stories she had begun devouring any book she could find.

"Now," Alfredo said to me, "she knows as many stories as you do."

I found this desire to equal me incomprehensible.

Exasperated in the end by my inability to approach her, I decided to send her a message. I had acquired a taste for enigmatic messages, for formulas enclosing several meanings at the same time. I whiled away several hours composing and destroying sentences. In reality, I didn't know exactly what I wanted to say, so hampered by ideas as I was. What's more, I was afraid of being tacky; in Lima I had an incurable fear of the ridiculous. At last, I came up with a formula that satisfied me. On a sheet of notebook paper, I wrote: "Every afternoon there's someone standing in the shade of a tree, awaiting punishment." Alfredo was my messenger.

Nothing in Leticia's behavior suggested that she had gotten or understood the message unless it was the glacial but nonetheless slightly distracted way she looked at me that night at dinner. I was worried that maybe my words hadn't been clear enough or that she wasn't smart enough. Even so, I headed for the river the next day and spent an hour mooning around the brush. It was only on the second day that I heard footsteps coming down the path. When I turned around I saw Julia spying on me. Julia was, in fact, a kind of private maid for Leticia, because in San Gabriel, as in a small kingdom, the master's daughter needs a lady-in-waiting. Her presence alarmed me, and after chasing her through the alfalfa field I managed to knock her down. Her small body was struggling under her full skirts, and I kept wrestling her, taking fiery pleasure in dominating her. She quickly stopped resisting, her muscles relaxed, and she remained defenseless, her cheeks on fire, her eyes closed. I noticed then that she had very fine features and that they were arranged so as to give her the look of a rare and beautiful animal.

"Who sent you here?" I asked.

"Miss Leticia."

I leaned over her until I felt her agitated breath on my hair. Making a keen effort, I got up and ran off with huge strides. When I looked back, she was still lying in the alfalfa, as if she had fallen asleep.

An unexpected event shook the residents of the hacienda that afternoon, and even I saw myself wrenched away from my affairs and confused by the general uproar. On account of the robbery, my Uncle Leonardo had undertaken an investigation, but it hadn't led to anything. For a while Jisha was a suspect and he was brutalized with such cruelty that even though I couldn't stand the sight of him since our fight, I felt sorry for him. Then it was the night watchman who suffered the humiliation of being accused. But it was clear that neither of these two household servants had anything to do with the crime. That was when my Uncle Leonardo began to suspect Engineer Gonzales. The robbery had taken place precisely during his stay, and when he found out about the engineer's coming trip to Lima and the money he needed for his marriage, his suspicions grew. I greeted this rumor with indignation and continued to believe, at heart, that the thief was Daniel, who had become the agronomist's most serious detractor.

The fact is, hoofbeats echoed on the patio and a mare, harnessed but without a rider, soon came trotting in. Stopping in front of its stable, it began shaking its head in an attempt to free itself of the bridle. It was the mount that Gonzales had left on six days before.

Masters and servants gathered immediately around it and there was no end of speculation. The most likely thing was that the mare had bucked off its rider on a bad stretch of road. But Daniel put forward that Gonzales must have abandoned it so he could go down the Huaylas gorge to Lima with the loot. Felipe behaved very forthrightly and said that if his friend didn't show up that afternoon he would go look for him. He might have fallen in a ravine.

Three hours later, Felipe, Leonardo, and the Negro Reynaldo saddled their horses and set off down the track to Cabana carrying ropes and lanterns. I wanted to go with them, but Felipe, who looked worried, was against it. I had no choice but to take refuge in Jacinto's room and talk the incident over with him.

"Don't be alarmed," he said to me. "I know that road to Cabana very well and there are some hard parts. The mare must've thrown him and come trotting to the hacienda when it saw it was free. It's happened to me several times. Once I even broke two ribs."

As I was talking to him about the robbery and the rumors that were going around he went thoughtful.

"I don't know what to say to you," he replied. "That thing about the robbery seems ridiculous to me. Was there really a robbery? In any case, it's better to wait and not accuse anybody for now."

His answers struck me as excellent. I found him particularly lucid that night. Maybe it was because there was a full moon. For a few minutes he kept me entertained by talking to me about disquieting things. He said he saw in his dreams a face that was and wasn't his mother's. Then he talked about death in familiar terms, as a friendly rider inviting you up to the croup of his horse.

"When I die I'll leave you one of my rings," he said suddenly. "I've got three rings, my mandolin, and some old junk. I read somewhere that no matter how poor you are you always leave something when you die."

After I left his room I paced the hacienda arcades for a long time. The night watchman had already closed the gate, and he was walking around the cloister with his lantern in his hand. Jacinto's words had set off an avalanche of sad thoughts in my mind. I thought about my mother, about Lima, about things it was impossible for me to understand. I thought about other places, other countries where the sun never set. Only the thought of Leticia was able to cause me keen excitement. I saw her as one of my kind and I was attracted to her by what we had in common.

The moon had risen. I went into the drawing room and found Ema and the gringa arguing about something or other. I had no choice but to leave. My cousins were already in bed. I would have liked at least to talk to Alfredo or to Ollanta, whose wild and hypocritical look was beginning to intrigue me. Overwhelmed by loneliness, I wandered around the patio a little longer. When I got to the gate leading to the river, I saw a shadow sliding silently by. It must have been someone who was barefoot because there was no noise at all. When I approached I recognized the Indian girl Julia.

She had stopped against the wall with her hands together. I thought she was bringing me some message and I stood next to her for a long time, observing her with interest. Reaching over to her, I touched her cheek and I caressed her braid. I breathed in her smell, a mixture of filth and spearmint. For some reason, I got scared—maybe because the watchman was getting closer—and turning away I rushed to my bedroom.

I felt feverish, nervous, and without undressing I began waiting for my Uncle Felipe's return. The dogs were barking furiously in the patio and around midnight I fell asleep. It must have been near dawn, or maybe it was the moonlight, but when the door opened a subtle clarity invaded the room. At length the light came on and I was able to see Uncle Felipe. He was sweaty, his clothes were ripped, his boots covered with mud. He lit a cigarette and stood still under the light bulb, not bothering to take off his hat. His eyes, in a slight squint, were looking at me without seeing me.

"So?" I asked, getting out of bed. "What happened?"

"We've brought him in now," he answered slowly.

"Is he asleep?"

"They're dressing him now. You'll see him tomorrow. At the wake."

I froze. Felipe's hands were covered with layers of black. He poured water into the washbasin and started washing them.

"Is he dead?" I asked.

"Yes!" he shouted, turning around abruptly. "He's dead! He was killed! Somebody hit him in the head with a pick four times and then they threw him into a ditch. Is that what you wanted to know?"

My Uncle Felipe's expression frightened me as much as the news itself. Retreating, I fell seated on a trunk, fighting that feeling of nausea, of a freeze-up in the brain that, when I was a schoolboy attending mass, always came before a long dizzy spell. Felipe kept observing me for a while, his jaws firmly set, a gleam in his eye. Then he went back to the washbasin and wet his head, his arms. When he finished rinsing off he sat down on the edge of the bed and went quiet. I didn't dare ask him anything else. Then I saw him go to a corner and grab a little suitcase that Gonzales had left there to pick up on his return. Inside, there were ties, combs, pictures. Felipe took a packet of letters and starting flipping through them distractedly. At times he would pause over one and skim it all the way through. They must have been his fiancée's letters.

"What good is all this?" he murmured in that caustic tone he always used for other people's feelings. "What's the point of all these words? Listen: 'I've missed you a lot.' 'When we get married.' Bah! What a bunch of lies! A waste of time! You want to complicate your life! All this is idiotic!"

For a long time he kept reading and making scornful comments on the letters. At times, violent indignation made him raise his voice or laugh bitterly. He got so worked up that he scolded me, threatening me with a fist, as if I were partly to blame for all these events. Finally, he ended up throwing the letters in the back of the suitcase.

"One more dead man down the hole!" he shouted. And dropping dressed onto the bed, he went still, facedown, as if he had passed suddenly from stormy vigil to the deepest sleep.

THE INNOCENTS

*T*he wake took place the next morning. That same afternoon he was buried in the San Gabriel cemetery, which was on top of a small hill near the aqueduct. The priest had come to Mollepata to celebrate the funeral rites. The coffin, which the carpenter Tobías had made in a few hours, was carried by some of the hacienda laborers. Before they reached the cemetery, Felipe offered to carry it for a stretch. The women were wrapped in large dark shawls that gave a sad look to their eyes. When the priest was intoning a psalm, before the first shovelful of earth, a heavy storm broke, so he cut short the sacrament and gave his blessing with a quick wave of the hand.

I could hardly manage to cast a glance at the body that morning. We young people weren't allowed to see it. He had been dressed in one of my Uncle Leonardo's old suits. His face was wrapped up in a white cloth. His belongings, which were very few—his big suitcase had disappeared—were made into a package and sent to the Trujillo address that was on the back of his letters. In addition, my Uncle Leonardo wrote a short letter mentioning the crime.

The first inquiries into the murder got underway. A telegram was sent to Santiago, and that very night two civil guardsmen arrived, their big horses exhausted and their rifles sheathed in their saddles. That's how I managed to find out some of the details about the murder. On a stretch of road between Mollepata and Cabana, land belonging to an Indian community, some peasants had found the dead man. Once the news had gotten around, it wasn't hard for my uncles to locate the body. A pick, blood-stained at the tip, was found at the site of the crime. The victim had been robbed of his wallet, his watch, and his suitcase.

The civil guardsmen rested in the hacienda, and supplied with brandy by Leonardo they went on their way. In that lost mountain valley whose name didn't even show up on maps, the only justice people knew was police justice. It was the civil guardsmen who extracted confessions, determined guilt or innocence, kept note of the proceedings; and only after a long delay did the correct jurisdiction get hold of the matter, which was by then often so complicated that it was necessary to start the inquiry all over again or proceed with the one already started at the risk of following a false lead. So judicial errors were frequent, and it often happened that many years after a defendant had been sentenced, the true criminal was found. These discoveries would disconcert the judges in the provinces, and since they couldn't call a new trial for the same crime or face bringing upon themselves the embarrassment of annulling the results of the first one, they had to let the real criminal go or invent some crime to justify his arrest.

For days the murder was the only topic of conversation in San Gabriel. Everybody was upset, and when my uncles went out to inspect the fields they did so armed to the teeth. Security at the hacienda was stepped up, and a new watchman was put by the back door. At meals, tales of murders and bandits were told. There was talk of the Benel brothers, who had laid waste to the region between Jaén and Cajabamba. Then the conversation merged into stories about lost souls and apparitions. I noticed then the fund of superstition in the heart of the provinces. Even the most serious people believed blindly in these phenomena, and they had all had some experience that left no room for doubts. Leonardo told how his brother Aníbal, who was hundreds of kilometers away, had appeared to him moments before his death and kissed him on the cheek. In these conversations, which even the servants joined, voices went hollow, candles were lit on the cupboards, people walked on tiptoe, and it all seemed to form part of a very ancient rite that the pagan forces of the planet participated in.

Leticia, infected with the temper of her caste, took part in these chats with the fervor of an initiate. I never saw her eyes so dark, so impenetrable: fear gave them supernatural depth. The crime had resulted in a truce between us, and several times she surprised me by turning to me and telling me a story as if I were an outsider or, on the contrary, a long-time confidant. Only when she noticed that my attention was focused more on her face than on her words did she interrupt herself, turn toward the person sitting next to her, and go on with her story.

All these events coincided with Jacinto's relapse into one of his periodic fits of melancholy. As in the first days of my stay at the hacienda, he kept to his room, playing the mandolin off and on. One of the cooks brought him food that he would push under his bed without tasting. Even so, he often went out to the patio, ordered a horse to be saddled, and galloped off toward Santiago. Nobody seemed worried about his departures.

"There goes Jacinto," they would say, looking out the window.

An hour later he would be back, his head sunk into his chest. Leaving his horse in the hands of a laborer, he'd drag himself to his room. When he was really late, my Uncle Leonardo would pull on his poncho and go out to get him. Soon after, he would bring him in riding on the croup, half-drunk, from a tavern a few leagues away from the hacienda.

Sometimes he drank too much and came back singing or yelling insults. Jacinto had many forms, and I was amazed to discover new aspects of his character every day.

One of those days I managed to get into his room. I found him as I had first seen him: his hat on, a seven-day beard darkening his face. He didn't seem to know anything at all about the murder.

"And you say he was buried with boots on?" he asked. "With the damp his feet will swell and they'll burst open under the ground."

After one of his flights toward Santiago, Leonardo was getting ready to go after him, and because I happened to be around he asked me to go him. In reality, because there was something about him that intimidated me, his brow maybe, or his definitive adulthood, I spoke little with Leonardo. For a long time we advanced together slowly and in silence. He was looking at the toes of his boots. But now and then he raised an eyebrow to cast a furtive glance of clandestine love at the hacienda lands.

"I might have to give all this up one day," he suddenly said to me. "That little grove where the three of us used to play at bandits when we were seven years old...."

A league farther on, he said:

Here and in a lot of other places, farming is a gamble. Until the moment of the harvest you don't know if you'll line your pockets or if it'll all go to hell. I have ten hectares sown with potatoes and every night I tremble with the fear that it's going to freeze. Besides, it's getting harder and harder to get labor. It seems like the Angasmarca people are going to work for Don Florencia Huertas or Don Evaristo this year. I have to win them over with gifts. Last year I built them a chapel. I don't know what the head of the villagers will ask me for this year."

Then he added:

"Sometimes I feel like selling the land and moving to Lima. I can buy a few little houses there and live off the rent."

"And what will you do about Alfredo and Ollanta?"

"They have no interest in the land. They'll ruin all my work. Alfredo worries me most of all. Hasn't he seemed a little strange to you? Sometimes he hangs around me as if he wanted to say something, then he runs off. Ever since he found out I'm going to send him to Santiago, he hasn't said a word to me. And Leticia is another problem! I can't wait until she gets married."

Those last words chilled me.

"To Tuset?" I asked shyly.

"Yes, to Tuset. He's a good kid, even if he's still a bit unrefined. But I don't think Leticia loves him. I haven't talked to her yet. Has she said anything to you?"

I went red, and my uncle looked at me with curiosity.

"What, has she talked to you about it?"

"No," I answered dryly, not opening my mouth again.

In any case, we had made it to the tavern. Jacinto's horse was at the door. When we went in we saw him with his elbows up on the table, a huge can of chicha in front of him, surrounded by several Indians whose drinks he had probably paid for. This time he behaved with docility and let himself be led away without protest. Leonardo put him up on the croup and took the road back to the hacienda. I went back angry, splashing through puddles on purpose and destroying clumps of Spanish broom.

When I went into the patio I was determined to talk to Leticia. In vain did I search all the rooms in the house. I remembered that one time after I had looked for her all over I saw her reappear with some straw in her hair, so I ran up the stairs to the loft.

Between the ceiling of the rooms and the roof of the house was a vast space where you had to walk bent over to avoid hitting your head on the roof-beams. Seeds, grain, fodder, old harnesses, and useless junk were stored there. A few small windows facing the road let in light. That place, which served as storeroom and granary, was known to everybody as the loft.

After going through several compartments I ran straight into Leticia, who had gotten up from her pile of hay when she heard footsteps. She had a wooden knife in her hand.

"Don't take another step or I'll stab you!" she shouted, raising her arm. "What did you come up for? I'm the only one who can come up here."

Her threat, far from terrifying me, redoubled my valor, and twisting her wrist I got her weapon away from her. As I was about to throw it out the window, she spoke up:

"No, please, don't be cruel! Don't throw away my knife! It took me three days to carve it!"

I just threw it into a corner.

"I want to talk to you," I said resolutely.

After picking up her knife, she sat down on the load of hay. My firmness must have surprised her. She ran her thumb slowly and completely over the blade of her knife.

"What do you want?" she asked, looking at me with that insolence that usually hid her fear.

"You can't marry Tuset."

She jumped over to the window and put her head out. I saw only her waist, her hips, prey to a spastic movement, as if she were laughing out loud to the road. Finally, she turned around. She was very serious. Her brow—Uncle Leonardo's brow—was exaggeratedly furrowed.

"Tuset is very nice and I love him a lot. At the end of the year we're getting married."

"That's not true!" I protested furiously.

"Why not? What does he lack that other people have? Besides, he's rich. This very night I'm going to talk with my father."

I stood looking at here with hatred, tempted to jump on her neck and start hitting her. She must have noticed what I was thinking, because she went extremely pale.

"If you do anything to me I'll shout," she said. "I'll shout so loud that everybody will come and beat you to a pulp for being a bully."

I turned my back on her and ran out of the loft. I slipped on the ladder and just about fell into mid-air. It was no longer hatred I felt but a savage zeal for destruction. I felt like shouting, like breaking things, like committing some act of cruelty. Near the ladder was Marica's room. I don't know how but all at once I found myself facing her. She was in the same chair as the week before, without having changed her position. You might think she hadn't moved that whole time. I pounced on her like a wild man, but one step before reaching her I stopped. On her face was such a look of absence that it calmed my fury. I realized that she wasn't there, that her body was only a pretext because her heart was beating years away. The peace and the infinite calm of her face dehumanized her, turned her into something abstract such as an idea or a prayer. My knees folded, and all at once I found myself leaning on her lap, my gaze fearless, as if on the edge of my own grave.

Toward dusk hoofbeats were heard on the road, the hacienda dogs started barking, and soon afterward the civil guardsmen made their appearance. From the saddle of one of their horses extended a rope at the end of which an Indian, tied by the waist, blood all over his sandals, was struggling to keep up with the animals.

Right away, everyone in the hacienda, Felipe and Leonardo in the lead, crowded around him. I pushed my way through and made it to the front row.

"We've got him!" shouted one of the guards.

That's when I managed to take a look at the murderer. He was repulsive. His shirt was soaked with sweat, his vest buttonless. His hair fell over his forehead like a woman's bangs and his slightly crossed eyes looked stupidly around him. A trickle of green slobber was trailing from his open mouth.

"This is a fellow who hasn't done his military service, either," added the other guardsman. "He doesn't have any papers and he's trying to pass himself off as an imbecile. But it's just a trick, since he sings and even dances the *huayno* when he's with his wife and nobody else can see him."

"Has he confessed?" asked Leonardo.

"Not yet. He won't say a word. But half a league from his house we found a suitcase strap that might belong to the victim. Here it is." The civil guard took out a strap eaten away by the weather. Leonardo examined it and passed it to Felipe.

"We'll halt tonight and head for Santiago tomorrow. We're really exhausted."

The prisoner, who had bent down until he was in a squat, was panting like a cornered animal. Shaking his arms, he began grunting, pointing at the guardsmen. With his huge hands he pounded his chest and shook his head no.

One of the guards pulled on the rope.

"There he goes again with his tricks. That's one sly half-breed! Insolent, too. He threw himself to the ground on the way and we had to drag him.

I saw then that the knees of his corduroy trousers were ripped and his elbows bruised.

"Take him to the dungeon," ordered Leonardo.

In San Gabriel there was a dungeon. It was one of the rooms facing the patio, which I had walked in front of several times without know what it was for. The door had thick bars made of the trunks of eucalyptus trees. The prisoner was pushed in and the door was bolted shut.

"Let's go have a drink," said Leonardo, and the guardsmen followed him.

I remained for a minute gazing through a crack at the criminal's eye. It was an irritated and terrible eye that filled me with stupor, because it seemed to me that instead of one person looking through it there was a multitude of desperate people.

A Big Decision

*T*hree weeks went by. I remember them as the most withdrawn, the most meditative of my stay at San Gabriel. The previous events had deposited their larvae, and my heart was beginning to rot.

It was, first, the agronomist's death that taught me to view life as incoherent spectacle. I still remembered him talking to Felipe about his marriage, about the happy future awaiting him. Some time earlier I had experienced the death of my mother as an irremediable rending, but that death came slowly, as the corollary to a long illness, after having shown its visiting card. The agronomist, on the other hand, had fallen at a bend in the road with all his dreams intact. I thought that he might have had children, that he might have been happy, that he might have deserved it. Now he was decomposing in foreign ground with nobody to remember him. No response had come from Trujillo to the letter my Uncle Leonardo had sent. Several times I went to the cemetery, whose calm space attracted me. It was a rectangular plot surrounded by walls with a cross on each corner. The wooden gate, always open, called you in. Its hinges creaked in the silent country and startled flocks of wild birds. You could see leaning crosses with sad wreaths like necklaces and only one tombstone: Leonardo's father's. Death was beautiful in that remote plot. I would return from those walks with a great emptiness in my heart and an invincible desire to curse the heavens.

The capture of the prisoner, second, increased my distress instead of allaying it. I suspected he was innocent. The very night of his confinement, my Uncle Leonardo gave me a lantern and asked me to go with the guardsman to the dungeon. When we went in, the Indian was lying on his back, his hands tied, on the bench running along the wall. The guardsman was bringing a pitcher of chicha and a piece of bread. All at once, he dropped them and kicked them with his boot.

"So you're playing the imbecile?" he shouted. "Just wait until we get to Santiago!"

The Indian only grunted. One of the cooks recognized him and said he was Seferino Trigo, deaf-mute from birth. In the highlands, justice was generic. Individuals didn't matter. It was presumed that an Indian had killed a traveler, so it was necessary to bring an Indian to Santiago; which one didn't matter. The guardsmen were mestizos with authority who hated the villagers—free Indians—as much as they hated white people—landowners with power.

What's more, the image of Leticia had infiltrated even my dreams.

Her decision to marry Tuset filled me with anger, perplexity. After our talk in the loft I would see her walking around the house, and in my eyes rancor strangled desire. She had tied the wooden knife to her waist and wouldn't even put it away at mealtimes, saying it was to "defend herself from murderers." But I was sure that she was afraid of me, that she was spying on me. Julia was always around, following my every step.

During those days, I didn't talk to anybody but Jacinto and Alfredo. The former had recovered from his depression and was diligently carrying out the little chores that made up the greater part of his obligations: supervising the milking, going to Mollepata for cigarettes. For something to do, I accepted his offer to teach me the mandolin. He stated enthusiastically that I had "potential." I started experiencing a certain pleasure in running the tortoise-shell pick over the strings. But I soon got bored, since I was bored by everything I didn't experience as a passion.

Alfredo, for his part, was worrying me. He looked more and more transparent, more and more fearful. His ears looked like onion skins and light filtered through them. Out of pity I decided to talk to Leonardo one day and I told him that I could teach his children and that he could send them to Santiago later. After examining my report cards, which showed that I had excellent grades, many of them faked, Leonardo agreed.

So began my brief professorship. Classes were after lunch in the dining room. I talked to them without any organization about history, geography, and botany as memories from school came back to me. Alfredo listened with his eyes open wide in admiration. But Ollanta started playing with crumbs and would soon fall asleep. Leticia looked in from the doorway a few times, would stay for a while watching, make a face, and end up leaving.

In one of those classes, talking about the Inca empire, Alfredo asked me if the Indians who worked on the hacienda were the same ones who had formed part of such a powerful empire, and when I told him that they were, he argued that it couldn't be, because the Indians from the old days were warriors, strong, healthy, and today's were full of lice, didn't have shoes, and ate only "potatoes and quinoa."

I was puzzled; I didn't know how to answer him. Days later I thought about the matter and asked my uncles. My questions must have seemed scabrous to them, since they just gave me vague or stupid answers. Their reaction proved to me that they had become the guardians of a truth that they didn't dare reveal but that I would discover on my own one day when I saw how the hours fell there, fury on top of fury.

My Uncle Leonardo, meanwhile, was still anxious about the fate of his harvest. He was the only one in the hacienda who fully felt the problems of the land. Felipe was a mercenary without any sentimental ties to San Gabriel. He had worked in every province in Peru without putting down roots, and in the end it didn't trouble him to strike camp and head off in search of new horizons. But Leonardo meditated with a thermometer in his hand before going to bed, his eye on the dry cloudless sky.

What's more, the price of tungsten kept falling. The war was coming to an end. It was odd to see how we experienced that phenomenon in the hacienda. Thousands of kilometers from the battlefields, protected by an ocean, by virgin jungle, the war was a chess match for us, a splendid adventure story. When the newspapers came from Lima we would yank them out of each other's hands to read the headlines. There were impassioned arguments. Felipe supported the Germans. Leonardo, on the other hand, who had dreamed about Paris in his youth, loved the French, and his mouth watered talking about French women. I followed their arguments, taking one side as soon as the other. All the arguments seemed reasonable to me, but at the same time insufficient to help me form a conviction. My great worry was to know what the newspapers would talk about when the war ended, how they would fill those huge pages that for as long as I could remember I had always seen covered with battles and tools of destruction. Jacinto, whom I asked about the matter, responded with the clairvoyance that often characterized him:

"Bah! Don't worry! They'll talk about peace."

In the last few days new guests had arrived at the hacienda. Among others, two hacienda owners who were traveling toward the interior and the governor of Cachicadán. The latter was a pure-blooded Indian, but with a varnish of Creole that made him seem picturesque. All his teeth were gold and he wore a beautiful vicuña poncho. In addition, he was learned, funny, sly, terrible when he was arguing, pitiless when he wanted to make fun of somebody. He had been in Lima for a few years and spoke with cocksureness about several congressmen friends of his that nobody had heard of.

Cachicadán was a nearby village, famous for the hot springs that flowed from the earth at a temperature of seventy degrees Celsius. My Uncle Felipe would say that there was nothing better than a dip in those waters after a drinking binge. He also told the story of a friend of his who, going drunk to the baths, fell into a jet of boiling water and had been "cooked like a chicken."

My Uncle Leonardo had sent for the governor to obtain his influence in getting labor for the harvest. So he feted him magnificently. Besides the great feasts, he was given a fine mare from the stables, crates of oranges, the best smoked hams. I began to see that those provincial positions, apparently so insignificant, brought with them a chain of gifts that made them desirable. The governor promised everything and heaven too, said he'd talk with the head of the Angasmarca community, and that he'd let him know the results. The only one who didn't believe those promises was Jacinto.

"He'll say the same in all the estates around here," he said. "And when he has enough mares to make a herd he'll laugh out loud at us."

One afternoon Leonardo got a letter from Santiago. At dinner he let us know that Tuset was announcing his coming visit. I, who had raised a wall of minor and time-consuming occupations to protect myself from Leticia, found myself attacked in my redoubt; and my fears redoubled. Through Alfredo I found out that Leticia hadn't talked to Leonardo about her engagement, but Tuset's visit would hasten the event. What mortified me the most was the expression of joy on Leticia's face when she heard the news; and on the next day she started sewing herself a new dress.

Too weak to wage battle, I sought compensation in reading. I had already read all the books in the hacienda, including thick veterinary tomes that bored me. With the money I had saved—handouts from Felipe and Leonardo—I ordered a parcel of books from Santiago, and when they came I shut myself in my room and began living by proxy the emotions not offered to me by life. They were mostly Dumas novels. For several days I was enraptured by D'Artagnan's adventures, I was in love with Andrea de Taverney, and I learned about the Capeto dynasty through their palace intrigues and their musketeers. But my rapture didn't last long, and I often got lost in thought, the book open in my hands, convinced that real life was different, that in real life, for example, Porthos would never have become Baron of Pierrefonds. Real life was full of traps against which neither virtue nor heroism was of any use. People died without knowing why, lovers were betrayed, and the poor in spirit never saw the kingdom of Heaven. My despair was reaching its limits. That was when an unexpected event came to my aid, and I saw in it the possibility of deliverance.

In the hacienda carpentry workshop some complicated machines to sift the ore from the mine had been built. My Uncle Felipe was in charge of transporting them and he was going to leave in a few days. I begged him to take me with him. At dinner my plan took on importance and I told Leonardo that I was planning to stay a long time at the mine so I could learn about the job.

"You'll freeze to death," he answered me. "I'm used to it, and not even I can stand more than three days. There's no heater up there, not even a bottle of hot water. You've got to get into bed with a brick hot from the furnace."

All efforts to dissuade me were futile. I argued that I wanted to work, earn money. Finally, to please me, Leonardo yielded.

"We'll try it. Go for a few days, but if something happens don't blame me."

I started getting ready with the greatest rejoicing. In my suitcase I put all my warm clothes, the books I hadn't read. Jacinto gave me a pair of boots that were too small on him, which I started wearing a couple of days before my departure, already feeling like an important person.

On one of those busy days Alfredo came into my room. He was visibly nervous and seemed to be hiding something under his sweater.

"I'm going to give you this to keep," he said, giving me a packet. "Take it with you to the mine. But swear to me you won't open it."

I was used to Alfredo's strangeness, and promising him I would do as he said I put the packet in my suitcase. The attention required by the things I was doing soon made me forget all about it.

At last, it was the evening of the trip. All the energy I had expended had left me exhausted, and since we were leaving the next day at dawn, I went early to my bedroom. Stretched out in bed, I was looking at the shadows coming in through the window, multiplying, when I noticed someone by my side, observing me. It was Leticia. I was so surprised I shouted.

"Ssh!" she whispered. "I came in slowly because I thought you were sleeping." She withdrew toward the window.

My heart began to burn in my breast in such a way that I couldn't get up or open my mouth. Leticia had rested her hands on the windowsill and I saw her profile outlined against the dusk like a shadow player.

"I heard you got some books from Santiago," she continued. "And I want you to lend me some of them."

I jumped up and headed for the switch to turn on the light. In the darkness I stumbled into Leticia and I felt her hand grabbing my wrist. Her face was very close to mine, and in the shadows I could barely see its oval shape and her terribly big and liquid eyes.

"Don't go to the mine," she said, grabbing my other hand.

I was puzzled for a moment, not knowing whether it was an order or a plea, but then, obeying an ungovernable impulse, I took her by the waist and pressed her with such force that her body seemed to break in my hands. From her throat came a moan. I had the impression she was crying.

"I don't want to be left alone," she whispered, beating me on the chest with her fists.

I didn't know what to say. I kissed her hair, her breasts; all at once the light went on in Felipe's side. Leticia moved away from me and left hastily. She must have run into Felipe, because he appeared in the doorway and stood watching me with a funny look on his face as he practiced whistling a tune.

"Ready for the trip?" he asked.

I didn't answer. Without getting undressed, I fell into bed again. When I saw my packed suitcase I decided not to go. But at four in the morning, when Felipe woke up, I mechanically finished packing and was soon ready for the day's trip.

Day was just breaking when we left.

In the Hut

*M*y biggest decisions were always prompted by obscure feelings. I never knew for sure why I left for the mine. For a while I told myself that getting away from Leticia was a way to approach her, since distance would only exacerbate my passion. I also told myself that it was time I did something useful, learned a trade, earned money for my work. Soon I began to suspect my departure was only a reprisal taken against my cousin for the minor slights I had received from her.

I remember that at one point of the trip I was about to turn back. Half an hour from the hacienda, I looked back and saw the red tiles of San Gabriel on the valley floor. The premonition that I would never return oppressed me and I reined in my mule violently. Felipe, who was going ahead, spoke to me, and I resumed the march with my head down.

The difficulties of the route soon demanded my attention and distracted me. First, we went through very dense woods where we had to use a machete. Daniel, who was also one of the party, loaded his rifle, saying that there were bears and mountain lions around. At the rear was the muleteer, who was leading two mules with the sifting machines.

After the woods we started climbing the slope of a mountain whose summit was lost in the clouds. Felipe said to me that the mines were "up there." It seemed impossible to me that we could climb that parapet where there was no path to be seen. The mule track we were on was so narrow we had to travel in singe file. To our left, a deepening abyss.

We made it finally to a place where all trace of vegetation disappeared. We were riding on bare rock. The abyss had doubled in depth and at the bottom you could see a green lake with still waters. Daniel told me a rock took a minute to reach the lake. He was in a good mood that day and he offered me cigarettes, which I refused.

When we got to the hardest stretch, Felipe was in front, Daniel in the middle, and I at the rear, all of us close to one another. That was when something happened that almost had fatal consequences. Could it have been an illusion? I was riding a little distractedly, but it seemed to me I saw Daniel leaning over the neck of his mule, reaching forward with his arm. Suddenly, Felipe's mule reared, made a strange movement, its rear legs wavering an instant over the abyss and only by a miracle, scraping the bare rock, did it manage to stay on the path. For a minute Felipe was breathless, hugging the neck of his animal. When he turned around he was incredibly pale and had purplish rings around his eyes.

"I saw myself at the bottom of the gorge," he exclaimed, trying to smile.

"It must've had a splinter in the hoof," said Daniel coldly, pointing at the mule.

I started thinking. I remembered that outing to the duck lake when a stray bullet from Daniel's gun brushed Felipe's shoulder. A series of things became suddenly clear: the message Felipe had sent to the gringa, Daniel's sudden drunken return, the looks exchanged by these three people at mealtimes, the secret rivalry between my uncle and the accountant, between the gringa and the other women at the hacienda. Recovered, Felipe went on his way and began singing to get rid of his remaining fear. But Daniel had gone quiet. It was only when we got to the mine that, examining the mule's haunch, I discovered an imperceptible burn made with the tip of a cigarette. I said nothing for the moment. I still didn't think I had enough proof.

But the next day, before he headed back to San Gabriel, Felipe came to give me some advice and say goodbye.

"When you get bored, come back," he told me. "But do what you can to hold out a few weeks. That way you'll show Leonardo you're a man. I might come up in two weeks. Any messages for the hacienda?"

"Felipe!" I exclaimed, unable to restrain myself. "Watch out for Daniel!"

"Why?" he asked, surprised.

"Your mule has a burn on its haunch!"

Felipe went serious and examined me severely.

"I don't like observant people," he replied, leaving the shed.

I followed him until he mounted his mule. Daniel was waiting for him at the trailhead.

"You go ahead!" shouted Felipe. "I'll catch up at the gorge."

My eyes must have expressed anxiety.

"Relax," added Felipe. "Nothing's going to happen. Don't you have a message for Leticia?"

I tried to discover if that question had a double meaning, but Felipe had already started laughing. He messed up my hair with a slap.

"I'm going to give you some advice," he said. "Women are like fruit on a tree. I mean that only the ripe ones fall into your arms. The others, you have to reach out and grab them."

Immediately afterward, he spurred his mule and rode out of sight without looking back.

That's when my unreal, unforgettable life as a miner began. I call it that even though my job consisted of riding around the mine, monitoring the work in the galleries every now and then, and, very rarely, giving the miners a hand sifting the ore. For that work my Uncle Leonardo paid me a salary that he deposited in the hacienda safe.

Right off I made friends with the foreman whose hut, which was the only habitable one, I shared. He was a mestizo about sixty years old, deaf as a brick wall, and on top of that missing three fingers on his right hand. When he was young he had been a carpenter until he became useless for that job and had to find another way to earn a living. My Uncle Felipe had found him wandering around Lima and, moved by his fate, enlisted him as foreman. His tasks as foreman were, however, very limited and he spent most of the day in the hut freezing to death, cursing the Indians, missing his wife, who lived in Lima, and looking over and over again at the pictures in some old newspapers that he already knew by heart. He wore a scarf wrapped around his head and covering his ears, a get-up that gave him an exotic look. He never took off his heavy, worn-out overcoat, not even when he was sleeping.

My arrival delighted him, since he would at last have somebody to talk to. At first I had problems making myself heard, but then he got used to the movement of my lips and it became easy to communicate.

When he found out that one of my plans was to become foreman, he showed a different face, but then he started ranting about his job, saying he was sick of this exile and couldn't wait to be back in Lima, in short sleeves, walking in the sun. I lent him some novels I had brought, but I noticed they didn't much interest him. They would fall out of his hands. Later, he admitted to me he didn't know how to read.

The hut was small and it was full of crates and tools. There was also a large supply of coca leaves and brandy, because the miners were paid part of their salary in kind. As I was surprised not to see a stove, the deaf man pulled up the cowhide rug on the floor and showed me a trap door.

"Under there's the dynamite store," he said. "It's dangerous even to light a cigarette in this hut. The worst is that we can't keep the dynamite anywhere else or the Indians will steal it. You don't know them. You've got to keep your eyes open."

From then on, every time there was a storm and lightning flashed around the hut, I saw the foreman jump out of bed and, wrapped in his blanket, pace cursing from one end of the room to the other, spying out the window at the rain and casting terrified glances at the cowhide.

"One of these days we'll get blown to bits," he exclaimed, making the sign of the cross.

It was soon afterward that I began to take an interest in observing the miners. The mine was small and it was worked by about forty miners, all of them Indians from the region. Work methods were rudimentary and the ore was extracted with crowbars. There were no regulations or schedules of any kind. When the deaf man woke up he pulled a cord hanging over the head of his bed and a bell outside started ringing. A quarter of an hour later he would get up to see if the miners were ready. He would merely insult the slowpokes or threaten not to pay them their wages for the day. The hour work ended in the evening depended on the weather, or more unpredictably, on the foreman's mood. If his stumps were hurting him that day or if his longing for Lima was more powerful, it could get dark before the bell rang.

I had made some attempts to approach the Indians. Their reserve, their apparent submission, stimulated my curiosity. I often visited the shelters they built out of the local rock. They slept on the ground, on lamb fleeces or woolen ponchos. Some had brought their wives, who spent the day spinning yarn, cooking, or helping their husbands. When the women saw me they laughed at me, pushed each other, talking all the while in Quechua. The men, on the other hand, viewed me with suspicion. Very few of them spoke Spanish and not one had ever seen the ocean. Sometimes I would have a drink of brandy with them and see their faces liven up. But then a cold reserve came over them and I saw only their slanted eyes, set over their hard cheekbones, posed impassively on me. I felt then that I would never be able to understand them, nor they me. It wasn't just language and customs separating us but hundreds of years of culture. And there was something else: my apparent position of authority. I was one of the "masters" from the hacienda and even though I was doing them no harm for the moment, their instinct warned them that one day, bearded, invested with power, I could easily become their oppressor. Things weren't going to turn out that way, but it was a possibility, and that possibility alone was enough to put us in a constant state of cold warfare.

One of the effects of that life was that little by little I forgot about San Gabriel and its inhabitants. A few times I thought with sympathy about Jacinto, Alfredo, and Felipe, whom I considered brave despite his corruption. I wondered what he was doing, if he ever thought about me.

As for Leticia, I did all I could not to think about her. To drive her from my mind, I came up with flaws for her or exaggerated the ones she already had. I told myself that her voice was shrill, like Aunt Ema's, or that her brow would get wrinkled like her father's.

But in the fourth week, a surprise visit from Jacinto and Leonardo awoke a flood of memories and left me disturbed for several days. They were only there for a few hours, but I didn't stop bombarding them with questions. Leonardo had come to bring the money for the miners' pay. Among other things, I found out that Daniel and the gringa had left San Gabriel in confusing circumstances that Leonardo didn't clear up.

But the big news was the arrival of Lola, Leonardo's oldest daughter. She had been at the hacienda for two weeks. Jacinto talked about her with unwonted enthusiasm.

"You should come down to meet her. She's a very good girl. Felipe didn't come because he's showing her around San Gabriel."

But I restrained myself from asking about Leticia. In the end, I couldn't take it anymore, and as if joking, I asked if she was still carrying her dagger.

"Not anymore," answered Leonardo. "She turned sixteen and she's grown a little, even though she's still thin."

"And Tuset?" I added. "Has he grown, too?"

Leonardo laughed.

"He came the day after you left. He hasn't moved from the house since then. He and Leticia are going to exchange rings soon."

I didn't open my mouth again for the rest of the morning. Leonardo, on his mule, ready to go back, congratulated me on my stay at the mine.

"But it seems to me long enough," he added. "As a joke, it's over. It's time to come back."

But I was fervently against it and I said I wouldn't come down until the end of the year. I wanted to save enough money for a vacation in Trujillo.

"Then come down for Leticia's engagement," added Leonardo. And he left.

Days of anxiety followed. The foreman was astonished to see me lying in bed with my eyes fixed on the roof-beams. Wandering around me, he would ask if I was sick and wanted at all costs to play the witch doctor on me, since he had practiced witch medicine as a young man and was, so he said, expert at restoring dislocated shoulders to their place by putting an orange in the armpit.

To get away from him I would saddle my mule and ride into the wilderness. Above the mine were some absolutely untouched spots. There were no signs of life except for the high-flying hawks. The landscape, of such splendid solitude, seemed to me like a mirror that, for the first time, I could see myself in. My relationship to nature changed and a new voice seemed to resound in my ears. These were terrible moments when something within me was denuded, the possibility of hypocrisy was removed, and it was easy to realize that I was an imbecile or a predestinate or that I could easily and without hesitation take my own life.

One day I remembered it was my birthday, that I too was turning sixteen. What was I doing in that unwelcoming place?

I thought about Lima, about other birthdays with cakes, candles, shrill whistles, old, powdered aunts who left a silver coin in the palm of my hand when they said goodbye. Until eight at night, I kept my birthday secret, but a moment came when I couldn't take it anymore. The only person I could talk to was the deaf man.

"Today's my birthday!" I shouted, approaching him.

When he hugged me with his strong arms I cried like a woman. Then we drank a bottle of brandy, and stimulated by the alcohol, chatted until late at night. When I went to bed I was completely drunk.

I was liberated. Over the next few days I worked with the miners and recovered my calm. I began to notice, besides, that some of them, especially the younger ones, were beginning to trust me. I joked with them or traded Quechua words for Spanish ones the way you might trade toys or tokens of friendship.

Coming back one afternoon from one of those days, I saw two horses at the door to the shed. I recognized the San Gabriel harnesses. The deaf man was taking off the reins and unsaddling the animals.

"Got visitors," he said when he saw me.

When I went into the hut I saw Leticia and Tuset sitting on the bed, waiting for me.

END OF AN ADVENTURE

For a few seconds we stared at each other. Finally, Leticia stood up, and coming over to me with admirable naturalness, gave me a hug.

"You've changed," she said, giving me, just as on my first day in San Gabriel, a kiss on the cheek.

Her gesture served as an example for me and I struggled to act politely. After talking for a while, I felt sure of myself. Tuset, who seemed to be in a very good mood, explained to me the purpose of their visit. Besides wanting to see me, they had come for two reasons: to look over the mine—since Leonardo was thinking of turning the management of the mine over to him and he was interested in having it—and to let me know of his coming engagement to Leticia. Having been forewarned by Leonardo, I received that last bit of news with exemplary coldness.

"Congratulations," I mumbled.

"I hope you'll be there," added Leticia.

I promised to come down the evening of the celebration.

We kept talking for a while about unimportant matters. I had noticed that Leticia was starting to lose her cool as she registered the dry and expeditious tone of my replies. As the afternoon wore on and the conversation began faltering, I suggested a tour of the mine. The three of us left the hut.

As we walked, I looked at the riding outfit Leticia wore with such elegance. It was new and it was clearly part of that vast scheme of prenuptial fineries that women know how to manage with such coquettishness. What's more, she was making an effort to adopt the manners of a young lady, an effort that made me keenly sad. Sometimes I wanted to find again in her the boy in trousers who ran around the pastures and whose daring surpassed that of all the other boys around.

Tuset, meanwhile, was bombarding me with questions that I dispatched with the precision of an expert. We analyzed the ore, started the sifting machines, went down to the bottom of the mineshafts. Leticia was beginning to get bored.

"Go back to the hut if you want," he told her, and the two of us went on with the inspection. When it started to get dark we went back. On the way we ran into the deaf man and Tuset got into a conversation with him. I kept going.

When I went into the hut I saw Leticia sitting next to the table resting her chin in her hand, her gaze absent. My presence didn't make her blink. I stood hesitantly in front of her, not knowing how to take advantage of that momentary solitude. She didn't say anything either, and her eyes were looking me over with that distant expression of hers while her fingers were playing distractedly with the crop. Suddenly, from her barely open mouth, a whisper emerged:

"You're an idiot."

I took a step toward the table and she stood up quickly. The crop was swinging in her hand. Her pupils were on fire, her teeth were flashing with that ferocity that had terrified me once before.

"What do you want? Don't come any closer! I could whip you."

I stood still, my arms at my side. She slowly lifted her hand and the tip of the crop brushed my cheek. Then she started laughing.

"I scared you, didn't I? Did you think I was going to whip you? You're as pale as a soul in purgatory!"

Leticia had approached the window and was leaning on the sill looking at the country.

"Here comes Tuset," she whispered. "I can see him getting bigger little by little... he's shaking his head from one side to the other... tic, tac, tic, tac." She turned at once toward me: "Why did you leave? Why didn't you pay attention to me that night? The next morning I went into your room and burned all your clothes with a cigarette."

Tuset came in stamping his boots. His presence immediately transformed Leticia into another person.

"I'm a little tired," she said. "We should stay here until tomorrow."

Tuset was of the same opinion. He was interested in the mine and wanted to know even more about it. The three of us sat around the table. I opened a bottle of brandy and we started talking. A sudden enthusiasm compelled me to swallow torrents of drink. The discovery that Leticia reserved for me a primitive, fierce aspect of her character had restored to me unlimited confidence in my own strength. Just then I felt sorry for Tuset; I almost sympathized with him. Not to get left behind, he too was sipping his brandy without caution. He had gotten tipsy and was starting to talk about his plans. I saw something chimerical in those plans that kept me from believing them. I had eyes only for Leticia, who was struggling to share in her friend's enthusiasm. It often seemed to me that one glance was all it took for us to understand each other, that with one gesture we revealed thousands of secrets, and that we, with our silence, were the ones talking, and that Tuset, with his chatter, the one excluded from our intimacy. Stimulated by this idea and by the supplementary courage given to me by the alcohol, I resolutely put my hand under the table and took hers. Leticia's hand remained for a moment in mine, but soon I felt her nails gouging the back of it slowly and deeply. When I withdrew my hand I saw a pale track that was beginning to color. Then I remembered that halt in the shelter on the hill when I saw the same mark on Tuset's hand. And I wasn't mad at all; instead, I was oddly gratified. I realized that Leticia marked only that which, in one way or another, must belong to her.

It was finally time to go to bed. The deaf man got sent out to sleep in the tool shed and we began to suspect that it would be hard to accommodate ourselves in the two beds. In the end, despite my protests, Tuset insisted on sleeping on the cowhide so as not to deprive me of my bed.

I couldn't fall asleep until late. In the shadows I saw Tuset stretched out on the floor, and beyond him, the bed where Leticia was sleeping. A subtle fragrance, a mixture of the vapors from women's clothing, the mysteries of sex, permeated and enriched that miserable hut. Before I fell asleep it occurred to me that to approach Leticia I would have had to go over Tuset's body. In those circumstances, it seemed to me more than just a simple metaphor.

When I woke up the next morning—the sun of the bleak Andean plateau was streaming cold through the window—Leticia, playing the industrious woman, had already gotten up and was fixing breakfast. Her pale cheeks told me that her sleep had also been troubled. Tuset, on the other hand, was stretching on the floor with a great deployment of yawns. An hour later they were ready to go back.

As I accompanied them to their mounts, Tuset told me again that he was interested in the mine and that he would discuss it with Leonardo. Leticia, for her part, insisted that I come to the engagement ceremony. The farewell seemed too long to me. With a foot in the stirrup, Leticia suddenly remembered a message from Alfredo.

"He told me not to forget to ask you for the homework he asked you to correct."

I was baffled. What homework was that? Only after thinking about it for a long time did I remember the packet he had given me the evening of my departure. After going through all my suitcase I managed to find it. It was something like a book wrapped in newspaper. I remembered my promise not to open it, but my curiosity was too strong. Hastily, fearing that Leticia would come in and discover me, I undid the wrapping: a wad of wrinkled bills appeared. I didn't have time to count them; I didn't need to, anyway. The robbery, which had provoked so much conjecture in San Gabriel, was cleared up. After wrapping the packet up again, I tied a string around it and left the hut.

Leticia and Tuset left. I stood in the doorway watching them. Neither looked back.

The whole day I went over and over the small incidents of that unexpected visit. I needed to come up with a new plan of action. I had never seen Leticia so slim, so sure of herself, with such a rich store of the unexpected and of means of seduction. Tuset, on the other hand, had been reduced to dust in my memory. I had the feeling, before his departure, of having reconciled myself to him by virtue of his simplicity and good faith, but some of the particularities of his that came to my mind made him seem ridiculous to me, hateful. Several times, referring to Leticia, he said "my future bride." Other times, he had taken her by the chin with a mushy look on his face. I refused to believe in the spontaneity of those details and I saw in them an unusual emphasis directed against me. Sure of his fiancée, sure of his future, sure of his fortune, Tuset was the happy man on the eve of the crowning of all his dreams. To me it seemed admirable that a man could manage to be happy, but what I couldn't put up with was his throwing that happiness into my face, especially when that happiness meant the sacrifice of mine. Everything about his behavior was revolting. Just then I felt more than ever the need to prevent that engagement.

But I didn't know what means to use or on what terrain to battle. I knew perfectly well that my means were limited. Because of his age, his fortune, the deference awarded older people, Tuset had a considerable advantage over me. I could oppose him with nothing but my passion. But that very passion made me distrust myself. I wasn't sure I loved Leticia, nor was I sure she loved me. Our relationship had grown anarchically, unexpectedly. Besides, when I thought about my long-term future I didn't see Leticia by my side and I didn't feel the need for her to be there. And that particular seemed to me a revealing sign.

By nightfall I was exhausted. Working in the mine, saving money, seemed reasonable to me. For Leticia's engagement, which would take place within twenty days, I would go down and then return to my work in the mine.

The next day I got up early and worked ferociously. I went over the payroll, put the accounts in order, tried to make changes. I realized that work could take on the form of a vice, an awful drug. The deaf man was amazed by my activity. Looking around, I had found a place to build a stable and more sheltered quarters for the miners.

When I came back at noon I saw at the entrance to a shaft a sight that chilled my blood: one of the miners had blown off his left hand and half his forearm with a stick of dynamite. Above his eyes, he was missing a piece of the frontal bone. Blood was gushing out as if from a pump. His fellow miners were trying in vain to stop the hemorrhage. When they saw me they went silent, looking at me coldly. I got scared: it seemed to me I could read an accusation in their looks.

I ran to the hut and burst in like a madman. The deaf man had fallen asleep in his chair with a folded newspaper in his hands.

"A first-aid kit!" I shouted, shaking him. "Where's the first-aid kit?"

He woke with a start and told me there wasn't any first-aid kit, that all there was was a jar of Mercurochrome. Showing me his mutilated hand, he added:

"When I lost these three fingers there wasn't any first-aid kit, either."

I ran out of the hut without answering him. The nearest mining camp was an hour away. An hour for the return made two. Feverishly, I started saddling my mule. The deaf man, who had come out after me to see about the accident, came back as I was tightening the cinches. He laid a hand on my shoulder and said:

"There's no need."

I turned around and stood looking into his eyes. Maybe my expression surprised him, maybe he felt sorry for me, because he didn't dare say a word. It was the first time I saw him anguished.

"These things happen sometimes," he said, and turning his back on me he returned to the hut.

That same afternoon, as we were sitting in front of each other devouring in silence our dish of potatoes, I felt the food getting stuck in my throat. Something like a curse was on that meal that I had earned so easily. I jumped up and started throwing all my stuff into my suitcase.

"What's happening?" he asked, but I didn't answer him.

Half an hour later I was heading back to San Gabriel.

SEVEN DIALOGUES

When I arrived , all the lights were on in San Gabriel and a crowd of servants and people I didn't know were on the patio. It looked like people had been mobilized for a huge feast or to fight a battle. They were so busy that my entrance went unnoticed.

The first person I met as I went into my bedroom was Felipe. He was in front of the mirror, trimming his mustache. For the first time I saw him without his country outfit, wearing an elegant gray suit. My presence appeared to cause him an indefinable mixture of surprise and displeasure.

"What? Back already?" he asked, looking at me out of the corner of his eye. And he went on with his preparations without saying another word to me. He seemed different. In Trujillo, during the course of his nocturnal expeditions, I had seen him with a similar look.

"What's going on? Why are there so many people?"

"What are you calling so many people? It's that harvest time is coming and there's traffic on all the roads. We've got something like twelve guests," and dilating his nostrils, he added: "You should take a bath. You smell like a lamb." And putting on his felt hat, he left the room.

In effect, after my stay at the mine, I was completely filthy. Even though the sun had gone down, it was still warm, so I decided to bathe. In the hacienda the bathrooms were defective, and when someone wanted to take a bath he had to say so in advance so that there would be time to heat up some buckets of water that were used to fill a wooden barrel. I had gone through that absurd process several times but had in the end opted to bathe in the river. As I went through the gate on my way to the river I ran into Alfredo, who was returning from a solitary walk. He immediately hugged me and went down the hill with me. He was incredibly skinny and more dazed than usual. I recalled the matter of the robbery and tried to probe him, but he wouldn't say a word. Only when I told him his "homework" was excellent did he get angry and try to run off.

"You promised me not to open the packet. You don't keep your word!"

Grabbing him by the arm, I managed to retain him. He kept going against his will, without opening his mouth. I didn't ask him any questions at all, because I knew by then that those silences presaged sudden confidences. When we made it to the river I undressed while he squatted on the bank.

"You know Daniel left?" he asked me all at once.

"Yes, I know he left with the gringa."

"The gringa is a bad woman, but Felipe's even worse."

As I soaked in the current, shivering, he went quiet.

"Which of the two do you think is to blame?" he interrogated me again.

"To blame for what?"

"For everything. You should know all right. In the end everybody knew, even the servants. Felipe and the gringa were having an affair, seeing each other at night when Daniel was gone or drunk, they were kissing...."

"It's the gringa's fault."

"No! Why blame her? Felipe was chasing her.... I've realized that it's always the man's fault."

"And then what happened?"

"One afternoon the gringa showed up on the patio with her head bleeding and Daniel chasing her. She ran over to Felipe's room. She was half-crazy. Felipe came out and had to defend her. 'Why do you have to butt in on this?' Daniel was saying. 'Are you by chance her husband?' 'Well, yes, I am her husband,' Felipe said, and they started hitting each other. They couldn't fight on the patio because Leonardo and the women were shouting, so the two of them went to the woods, one walking next to the other, arm in arm, as if they were going on a hunt. They came back after an hour; no, Felipe came back carrying Daniel over his shoulder. Felipe was beat up, but Daniel's face was destroyed. He spent a week in bed. I think he had some broken bones, because he couldn't move his arms."

"So why did he go?"

"I don't know. Leonardo and my mother talked to him. To avoid more trouble it was better for him to leave. The gringa didn't want to go, but Daniel made her."

"Just as well all that's over. Now things'll be calmer at the hacienda."

"Just the opposite. Now Felipe's been left alone.... Felipe hates being alone. It drives him crazy."

"That's true," I replied, remembering his awful mood of our lonely days in Santiago.

"But do you think he's really alone?" As I questioned him, Alfredo stood up. I got out of the water and dried myself with a towel. Alfredo picked up a rock and pointed at a lizard.

"I'd smash him just like that," he burst out, throwing the rock at the reptile and running off in a flash without paying attention to my shouts.

When I got back from my bath I was about to go into the living room, but I decided to pay Jacinto a visit first. He was happy to see me, but in that way so particular to him, so odd, of expressing his emotions with isolated parts of his face. His eyes were laughing this time, but his mouth was set in bitterness. His face was lined and yellow and his hat was pulled down over his forehead. The electricity books were still lying on his table.

"I forget everything," he said to me. "Today I read a chapter and tomorrow I don't remember anything. I take notes on a sheet of paper, but then I lose the papers or can't decode them."

"Study something else," I suggested.

"Everything bores me. Even the mandolin! I haven't played it for two weeks. I don't know what's wrong with me. Have you seen Lola?" he asked suddenly.

"Not yet."

"And Felipe?"

"I saw him all dressed up."

"All the time! All dressed up! For a while now he hasn't been doing anything but getting dressed up. What for? A pair of pants and a pullover are all you need. But since Lola came he only thinks about looking elegant."

"You should dress up, too."

"Not me. I won't go to the living room tonight. I'll eat in the kitchen with the servants. The living room is full of people. Besides, I don't feel like talking. Will you see Lola? I want you to give her a message."

"About?"

"Nothing. She told me she wanted to learn the mandolin. But that was a while ago and she hasn't said anything about it since. She must've forgotten."

The living room was packed and I had trouble spotting Leonardo. A compact nucleus of hacienda owners and businessmen was surrounding him. There were middlemen and wholesalers from Huamachuco and Santiago. The governor of Cachicadán was there, too, with a staff— probably some badge of his position—in his hand. He was drinking brandy and arguing heatedly.

"I've already discussed it with them," the governor was saying, "but you should go talk to the villagers. Parián, the leader, has promised me one hundred twenty laborers including men and women, but I think you can get more. You offered a bull, but now they want a school."

"And how the hell am I going to get a school?" complained Leonardo. "The only thing I can do is give them the desks."

"It doesn't matter. That's a start. But it would be better for you to show up in person. I've seen Don Evaristo prowling around the village."

"That Don Evaristo is despicable," complained an hacienda owner. "He has enough money to bring harvesters from Chiclín, but he'd rather take away from us the little labor we have around here. Last year he took it from me and my oranges rotted under the trees."

"Will do," said Leonardo. "One of these days I'll go up to Angasmarca and talk to the villagers. But you should pave the way for me. If the good weather keeps up the harvest will be excellent and I'll need at least two hundred people.

Leonardo saw me just then and waved to me. Felipe and Ema were talking in a corner. I approached them.

"The temperature dropped two degrees today," Felipe was saying. "You shouldn't be so sure."

"Be quiet! There's no reason to tempt the devil," answered Ema. "Leonardo told me that if things work out this year he'll buy a house in Trujillo. That's the way to start. The year after, it'll be in Lima…."

Felipe seemed distracted. Ema saw me and pulled me aside, asking about the mine. Felipe withdrew. Ema kept talking to me, jumping from one topic to another without pause. That seemed odd to me, because we usually exchanged monosyllables. But as she talked she was looking around her and very rarely met my gaze. I felt as if I were just a pretext and I was sure that Ema was listening to herself talk or was talking for some reason that I didn't understand. It must have been that it didn't suit her to remain silent or that it suited her to pretend to be having a nice chat. At times she laughed out loud at anything I said, even if there was nothing funny at all about it, or she overwhelmed me with information I hadn't asked her for, altering her voice and making lots of movements with her hands. Suddenly, she went quiet. I turned around and saw a young and robust woman entering the living room. Her face reminded me immediately of another one I had seen somewhere.

"She looks like a painted monkey," whispered Ema, bursting right away into laughter and patting me on the back as she asked, "And what else, what else?" as if I had interrupted my telling of a funny story. I ignored her. I didn't take my eyes off the woman who had just come in.

Felipe was standing next to her talking low. When he saw me he called me over.

"I'm going to introduce you to Lola," he said, pointing to his companion.

I shook her hand and she looked me over with interest.

"I know you very well," she told me. "Alfredo, Jacinto, and Leticia have told me a lot about you."

It wasn't Leticia she looked like. Not Leonardo, either. But I knew that face.

"Jacinto gave me a message for you," I said.

"Jacinto?" she asked, surprised.

"It must be about the mandolin," broke in Felipe. "Let him go somewhere else with his music! We're sick of musicians. Learn something more useful. How to kiss, for example, how to make men fall in love with you."

"Poor Jacinto," sighed Lola.

"Don't be silly," replied Felipe. "He's happier than the rest of us because he doesn't know anything."

I was about to say something in Jacinto's defense when Leonardo and Ema approached.

"Looks like we need some drinks," said Felipe, looking around. "I'll go make something." And he headed for the dining room.

"You look very healthy," Leonardo told me. "So tell me about the mine."

I gave him a brief summary that he listened to with a smile. Only when I mentioned the accident did his expression change.

"Something similar happened last year," he responded. "They're work accidents."

"There should have been a first-aid kit," I suggested.

"It doesn't matter. Besides, I'm not interested in making any improvements. Tuset might accept the transfer. That mine is a pain in the neck. If he wants, he can open a whole pharmacy up there."

Felipe reappeared carrying a tray with several glasses of a dark drink. It was a cocktail whose recipe had won him a reputation. He alone knew what went into it. But one was enough to fell an ox.

Since I had gotten used to alcohol at the mine, I drank several shots without uttering a word. Conversation became lively. I was starting to enjoy social life again, the unpredictable exchanges, the pointless conversations. I was thinking that in the mountains the masters lived well, frivolously, plentifully, and that the only thing ruining them was the bad habits of some, the laziness of others, the carelessness of still others, and the ambition of the majority.

I was working on one of those drinks when Leticia and Tuset appeared. They were holding hands; their cheeks were flushed. When Leticia saw me she came up short in the doorway, but then she went her way with that control conferred upon her by her long experience as an actress.

"Our miner is back," she whispered, smiling.

I thought I had to be cold, and as long as we were in a group, I didn't say a word to her. I spent the whole time talking to Lola, trying to make her laugh. It wasn't hard: Lola was of an extraordinary mental simplicity and I had the feeling she was, all around, much less than Leticia. When I won her confidence, she embarked on a tedious description of her life in the Marañon basin, a description I heard out stoically.

Dinner was of an exaggerated liveliness fueled by the intervening spirits of drink. I was feeling a little dizzy and I saw my fellow diners through an opaque pane of glass. Leonardo, in a good mood, was directing the conversation and telling stories. Felipe and Lola were drinking private toasts. Tuset sat down next to me and I had to put up with his attentions. Since the announcement of his engagement to Leticia, he thought he owed me something and he overwhelmed me with friendly words that I didn't know how to return in kind.

Toward the end of dinner there was a strange accident. Lola shouted and fainted over the table. Felipe picked her up and carried her to her bedroom while the diners burst into commentary. People mentioned a seizure. Ema said it was the third in two weeks.

I was sent for a jar of thymol, then, next to the bed, I saw how Felipe rubbed her chest as Leonardo put cold compresses on her forehead. The exact moment of the discovery was only when she opened her eyes and blinked in the light: Lola looked just like the pictures Jacinto kept of his mother.

THE BIG HUNT

While I was gone an excursion had been planned to Huayrurán, a nearby valley abounding in deer. The day after my arrival, with the weather still good, it was decided that the hunt was on. Some twenty mounts were saddled and after the big breakfast the caravan set out. My Aunt Ema begged off, saying she wasn't feeling well. Alfredo didn't go either.

After going through the eucalyptus grove we took a path I had never been on. It was a gorge a river had once run through, but now there was only the dry bed. Brambles, cacti, prickly pear, and low shrubs that seemed to feed off the sun grew in the limy soil. A range of bright red hills whose slopes were our goal rose in the distance. As usual, Leonardo and his group were in the lead. Bringing up the rear were the younger people; Felipe and Tuset were riding next to Lola and Leticia.

The two sisters—Leticia was in a riding outfit—were resplendent. Between them there was a secret spirit of emulation. It was mostly Leticia who tried to dominate. She never let Lola get ahead of her and on the rough stretches she was always the one to take the initiative, and guided by an infallible instinct, lead the way through the most dangerous short cuts.

From the start I joined Lola and Felipe. Despite her fainting spell the night before, Lola looked fresh and happy. Felipe, by her side, wouldn't stop talking, singing. He seemed rejuvenated, squandering vitality a boy would envy. I soon noticed my presence bothered him. I knew his limits, his minor desertions, and in front of me he felt like an actor playing a false role. I had no choice but to hang back and seek Jacinto's company.

Far from comforting him, the beautiful morning had left him in a brush-stroke of sad light. For the first time I noticed that his rigid and discolored face looked whitewashed, had something of a death mask. He immediately started talking to me about the Huayrurán valley, but he didn't take his eyes off Lola.

"So did you give her my message?" he asked suddenly.

"Yes," I answered.

"What did she say?"

I didn't know what to say. It embarrassed me to transmit her tepid interest in those lessons.

"I don't think she has time," I said at last.

"She doesn't have time!" he shouted. "She doesn't have time, but to joke, to sing, to dance, she does! She's an idiot. She laughs at everything Felipe says…. But she rides well. Did you see? You see how she jumped that puddle?"

At a bend we caught up with Tuset and Leticia. My cousin had gotten permission from Leonardo to come armed and he had gotten her a small pellet gun that she had fitted in a bandoleer. When we went by a high prickly pear bush, she saw a red prickly pear fruit that was prematurely ripe and right away she wanted to eat it. Tuset dismounted to look for a stick so he could knock the fruit down. Since he was taking a long time, I approached the plant and, standing up in the stirrups, reached for the fruit. Its spines went into my fingertips. I recalled Felipe's advice just then and pulled hard on the fruit. When I got it down I gave it to Leticia, my hand stinging.

"Didn't you hurt yourself?" she asked me, looking at me in astonishment.

I cleaned out the spines in my hair, the way I had seen the Indians do.

"What does it matter?" I answered her.

"Of course it matters! Your hand can get infected and you can even lose your arm. I don't want to have one-armed cousins."

"You don't need my hands," I answered brutally.

Irritated, she looked at me and threw the fruit to the ground. Spurring her horse, she rode on ahead. Tuset, distracted, was still looking for a stick and I profited from his absence to follow Leticia. The chase inflamed me. She had left the path and was riding through the brush growing out of the limestone, raising a cloud of dust. Then I saw her trying to jump an adobe wall in her way. Her horse was resisting, pulling its neck up.

"Wait!" I shouted, and catching up to her I took her mount by the bridle.

We both looked over the wall: you could see a huge natural crevice. Leticia didn't start; rather, she stood contemplating the strange shape of that fissure splitting the gorge in two and climbing halfway up the slope.

"You should always obey me," I said, but by then Tuset was galloping up, radiant, with a beautiful prickly pear in his hand.

"Here's a better one!" he shouted.

Leticia, contemplating the fissure, seemed spellbound.

"Did you see how deep it is," she whispered pensively. "Look, Tuset, you can't even see the bottom. Maybe you can go through there to the core of the earth, where people say there's molten lead and fire.

How could it have been made? It would be great to throw yourself in headfirst.

"Amazing," mused Tuset, who, somewhat disturbed, started following her.

At noon we reached Huayrurán. On the bank of the river that was eating into the wall of the gorge was a dwelling with a stable and chicken coop. A mestizo came out to greet us, followed by his Indian wife and several children. He was a local smallholder and a friend of Leonardo's. His name was Don Casildo. Jisha had left San Gabriel an hour earlier than we had to warn him, and on the long table under the arbor were pitchers of chicha, chilies, and several dishes of toasted corn. All the riders had dismounted and were falling avidly upon these appetizers. Don Casildo said his wife was fixing some finger-licking good guinea pigs.

After a short rest, Leonardo decided to cross the river and set out after the deer. The Huamachuco businessmen and the governor of Cachicadán wanted to do the same, and emboldened by the chicha, they checked their shotguns and spurred their horses through the current. Felipe and Tuset stayed at the farmhouse, accompanied by the women.

Don Casildo was a guitar player, and while we waited for the hunters to come back he kept us entertained singing *huaynos* and muleteers' couplets. A small party soon got underway and stamping feet stirred up dust. Lola turned out to be an excellent dancer, making Leticia jealous. As she lifted her skirts to spin, she showed her round knees, burned by the sun, and the start of a robust thigh that Felipe couldn't stop looking at. The chicha was flowing in torrents and even Leticia was a bit giddy. Only Jacinto, hidden in a shadowy corner, remained depressed. At one point he came forward and asked Don Casildo for the guitar, and his fingers, strumming the strings, interrupted the noisy frolic with a long pained pause. We had all listened stupefied, and when Jacinto finished we applauded him so enthusiastically he got confused and left the room.

That was the signal to leave. Tuset and Leticia went in one direction, Felipe and Lola in another. I was left alone with the owners of the house and Ollanta. Lethargy followed hard on the euphoria. The afternoon air was heavy. Looking for a place to rest, I went out into the country.

Near the stable I ran into Jacinto sitting on an adobe wall, staring absently at the hills, from where, now and then, a blast resounded.

"It's a bad time to hunt," he mumbled. "You've got to go out at five in the morning, just at daybreak. That's when the deer wake up and start moving around the forest in pairs, in herds. The males go first, sniffing the way forward...."

For a long time he went on talking without modulating his voice, as if he were reciting a poem or a litany. Only when he heard laughter behind him did he stop.

"Who's that?" he asked.

It was Felipe and Lola disappearing into the peach orchard.

"Where could they be going? They shouldn't be allowed to go very far."

"Let them," I suggested.

"No, let's go look for them," he said, jumping over the adobe wall.

The two of us entered the orchard. Jacinto's nostrils opened wide and he took his slingshot out of his pocket.

In the thickness of the orchard we lost each other. I had been killing time picking a few freestones and soon lost sight of Jacinto. After wandering a long time among the fruit trees, I suddenly stopped short. I had heard a noise close to the adobe wall marking the edge of the orchard. Advancing quietly, I managed to spot Felipe leaning over the grass. Lola was lying on her back, her skirt pulled up over her thighs. Her hands were vigorously holding back Felipe's, but they couldn't stop the action of his head, which he was lowering in agile movements over her head. I spent a long time watching this game. Lola's resistance enervated me, as if I were putting up with it. I would have liked her to relax her muscles and go still the way Julia did that afternoon in the alfalfa field.... Footfalls made me turn around. It was Jacinto approaching.

"So here you are! Have you found them?"

I blocked his path.

"There's nobody there. They must've jumped over the wall."

"That's what I figured," he said, and turning around he started back with his head lowered.

A sparrow, singing on a branch, distracted him. Getting his slingshot ready, he pulled the band back and let go a perfect shot that destroyed the bird's wing. Picking up the bird, he held it in his hand and stood gazing at it, puzzled.

"It's not his fault," he whispered as I walked away.

When I got close to the house I heard Leticia talking to Don Casildo.

'So you don't think I can hunt, either. If my father had let me go, I would have shot a deer right between the eyes."

When she saw me she went quiet. She picked up the guitar and started playing with the strings. From the kitchen was coming the smell of a stew, stimulating the appetite.

"Where's Tuset?" I asked her.

"He fell asleep in the woods."

The chicha made him sleepy," commented Don Casildo, going into the kitchen.

When she found herself alone with me Leticia hung up the guitar and went out to the arbor with her gun in her hand.

"Where are you going?" I asked her.

"What do you care!"

Close to the house there were some hundred eucalyptus trees forming a dense grove.

"Stop following me," said Leticia, looking back at me.

But I caught up with her anyway.

"I want to tell you something," I began.

"You always say boring and stupid things."

"I came down from the mine just to make peace with you."

"Make peace? We haven't fought."

"Sometimes it seems to me we have…. Sometimes I think you hate me."

Leticia burst out laughing with such naturalness that I was disarmed.

"What a dreamer you are! I don't have time to hate anybody. And don't talk to me again! If you want me to let you walk with me, shut up." And she penetrated the small grove.

I followed a few steps behind her, hearing the fallen leaves crunch under her boots. She was walking cautiously, looking through the trees as if stalking prey. Suddenly, she brought her index finger to her mouth.

"There he is," she whispered, pointing at Tuset, who was lying against a tree trunk, his hat over his forehead, snoring peacefully away. For a long time she gazed at him with a petulant look that was almost an insulting word.

"I'm tempted to do something," she whispered all at once. "I'm tempted to shoot him with a pellet."

"Are you crazy?"

"No," she answered, raising her weapon. "I always mean what I say. I'm going to wake him up with a shot."

I froze: the movement with which Leticia aimed the gun was just as savage, just as unstoppable as that with which, minutes before, Jacinto had hit the sparrow. The family resemblance was immediately clear. When Leticia pulled the trigger and Tuset shouted, the gun fell from her hands. I turned my back on her and ran toward the house.

Felipe and Lola were coming back just then, with blades of grass on their clothes. My face must have expressed my alarm, because Felipe came toward me.

"What's wrong?"

"Tuset got hit with a pellet!"

Felipe walked quickly toward the grove. I remained in front of Lola. The gravity, the weariness of her expression, reminded me again of Jacinto's mother's. Those strange matches between faces and manners disturbed me. I thought I was hallucinating.

"I'm leaving," I said, heading for the stable.

"What? Aren't you going to wait for the hunters?"

"I'm sick of hunts," I added, and jumping on my mule, I took the San Gabriel road.

I reached the hacienda at dusk. The patio was deserted. Sitting under one of the arches, I tried to put some order into my feelings. Life in San Gabriel was starting to seem despicable to me. On the way I had made a series of resolutions that congenital inertia kept me from putting into practice. I thought I would have to spend a season in Trujillo. But Leonardo still hadn't paid me for my work in the mine. Maybe it was better to wait. Things might improve after Leticia's engagement.

The house was empty and I started walking through it. Its thick, silent walls, the half-light of the hallways, cast an unusual spell on me. It must have been built a really long time ago, probably in colonial days. The floor was brick, the doors worn and shiny. Several generations of landowners must have succeeded each other under that roof. Leonardo was only the successor to an old caste. In his gravity, in his manners, there was something of a surviving and desperate lord. Marica was the link to tradition. If she could have talked she would surely have told terrible stories.

Without realizing it, I found myself all at once in the loft. Under the pile of hay where I had once talked to Leticia, I found several strange objects: the wooden dagger, a pair of eyeglasses, pencils, and a notebook with drawings. I realized then that Leticia must have hidden those things there to keep them away from prying eyes. That place must have been a sort of enchanted tower where she went to relive her childhood dreams.

After I went down, as I walked by the dining room, I heard a deep sigh. From the doorway I spotted my Aunt Ema sitting at the head of the huge table, her chin resting in her hand. The evening light coming in through the balcony put her face in a play of shadow that made her look incredibly old. So withdrawn was she that she didn't notice my presence. Disturbed, I got out of there.

It had been dark for a long time when the noise of a procession of riders could be heard on the path. I peered out the window and saw the crowd of excursionists coming through the gate. Life was reborn in San Gabriel.

At dinner there was talk of nothing but the hunt, the three deer I had seen in the kitchen, their eyes glassy, thin red tongues appearing between white teeth. Tuset was excited. So that the pellet could be extracted from his arm, he had been given half a liter of brandy, and sitting next to Leticia, having forgotten about the accident, he was the happiest man of the night.

When, later, in the living room, the dancing was about to start, a figure appeared in the doorway. It was the deaf man, with his poncho torn and his scarf wrapped around his head like a bandage. As soon as Leonardo saw him he approached him and the two of them disappeared down the hallway. Soon after, Leonardo, his brow furrowed, reappeared and summoned Felipe. The two of them withdrew, arguing out loud.

THE SMALL REVOLT

Something serious must have happened. The next day, throughout the morning, Leonardo, Felipe, and the deaf man had a long discussion in the study. The deaf man was protesting, saying he didn't want to go back to the mine, and Felipe was overwhelming him with insults.

"Then I'll go! Then you'll see how to deal with those people. You've got to kick those miners around. Otherwise they'll be after us all the time."

Leonardo recommended calm, but Felipe wasn't listening to reason.

"Give the Negro Reynaldo a shotgun and the two of us will go up to the mine. Then there'll be a party, I promise you!"

The discussion went on until noon. Afterward, Felipe came into the bedroom with his face red. His efforts to elude my questions were in vain. His own excitement forced him to talk.

"The miners got drunk and tried to attack the foreman. He got scared and the first thing he did was jump on his mule and spur it down to the hacienda. I said so before: they're going to eat that deaf man alive. You've got to show them you're a man."

"So why did they attack him?"

"You don't know those people! When Indians get drunk they get annoying, just the way we do, but with the difference that there's more of them so it's worse. It must have been on account of the accident, during the wake."

I remembered that while I was at the mine the miners had asked me several times about the "Redhead," as they called Felipe. They all had a grudge against him. The violence of his character had left them with plenty of bad memories.

"The worst of all is that I've got a lot to do in San Gabriel," sighed Felipe. "But anyway, I'll go up tomorrow. One warning: don't say anything to the women."

Just before lunch, while I was out on the patio, Lola came up to me and took me by the arm. She looked worried, even though she was humming quietly to hide it.

"Let's have a talk," she said to me, leading me to her bedroom.

When we went in Leticia was lying on her bed with her hands under the nape of her neck. She had on an extremely light nightgown that clung to her body like gauze. She closed her eyes and pretended to be asleep when we she saw me.

Lola started talking to me about her life in Los Naranjos, as her mother's hacienda was called. As she did so, she leaned back on her pillow and assumed languid manners that confused me. Her eyes explored me in a friendly way, with almost maternal condescension. I felt bad in her presence, and I didn't stop looking at the way her bust rose each time a sigh interrupted her story. Above all, it irritated me that she considered me immune to provocation. I barely heard her. I saw her lying in the grass, the day before, under the peach trees; and I envied Felipe.

"What is it that's happening around here?" she asked me suddenly. "Why is everybody so nervous?"

"I don't know," I answered.

"Something must have happened. I heard someone say Felipe was going up to the mine."

"Maybe."

Lola realized my reserve was forced and she changed the subject. She started asking me about my life in Lima. I sensed that she was setting a trap for me.

"Do you know Aunt Herminia?" she said at last.

"I lived three months in her house."

"Is it true that she's pretty old? Felipe says she's older than he is and that it's a pain to be married to a fifty-year-old."

"Maybe. She has gray hair."

Lola went thoughtful.

"Felipe doesn't love her," she mumbled. "He says she swears all the time, that she spends the whole day screaming."

Ema came in just then. On her face was that mask of impertinence she always wore when she was determined to put her authority, her malice, or her bad faith into practice. For a while she paced the room in her high heels. At last, she went up to Leticia and started scolding her for still being in bed.

"Tuset's in the living room asking after you!"

Lola had gone quiet. In the ensuing silence, I felt violence and unease filling the air. I was tempted to leave, but at the same time as it repelled me the presence of the women retained me. I was curious to know what they might say to each other out of sight of the older witnesses.

"So how was the hunt?" asked Ema, addressing Lola. "You haven't told me anything."

"It was good," Lola answered dryly.

"You didn't cross the river, did you? Neither did Felipe.... Ah, poor Felipe, since the gringa left he's lost his aim."

Lola had gone red.

"That's the way men are," continued Ema. "When their women leave them they act like idiots. I think the gringa bewitched him or something like that. Ah, but that's right, you didn't meet the gringa."

"No," said Lola.

"She was a horrible woman. I don't know how Felipe could have fallen in love with her. That man has no taste at all. All his Trujillo women must be just as ugly. Isn't that right?" she asked, addressing me.

That she should involve me in her intrigues annoyed me.

"I don't know anyone!" I answered.

"Ah, you're playing the fool. So you want to cover for him, right? But I've seen pictures of them and Felipe has even read me their letters. In reality, I don't think he takes them seriously. He's just a womanizer."

Lola got up. Her face was livid.

"I'm going out to get some sun," she said, heading for the patio.

Ema watched her go out and when she lost sight of her she burst out laughing so hard she ended up crying.

"She's a sly one! And she still plays the innocent when she already knows how to eat with her own hands. I can't wait until she goes back to her mountains.... And those attacks of hers are a ruse. She fakes them to get chest massages and to get money out of her father...."

She went on talking for a while, first addressing me, then Leticia, who was still lying down, her eyes half-closed. When she saw the meager attention paid her words she left grumbling.

I stayed curled up in Lola's bed. Ema's act had astounded me. I had never seen her so out of control, accompanying her screams with such rude gestures. I would have liked to go out looking for Lola and show my solidarity for her, but Leticia's presence held me. The indifference with which she had witnessed the whole scene, not bothering to open her eyes, was alarming. I interpreted it as a sign of insensitivity.

"Things are going badly," she said at last, without moving from her bed.

"I thought you were sleeping," I said.

"You knew I was awake. Why are you lying? I saw you looking at Lola with your mouth open, then at my mother. They only thing you do is look. You looked at me too. It seems as if you've never seen a nightgown."

Getting up, she took a few steps around the room, then stood still, her arms crossed.

"Things are going badly. I noticed it a long time ago. Since you came. You've brought bad luck."

"That's why I'll leave here as soon as I can."

"That would be the best thing. But where are you going to go? Do you even have house? Sometimes I feel sorry for you."

I didn't know whether to believe her at that point. Experience had made me distrusting.

"Are you being serious?" I asked.

"I'm always serious. Do you remember yesterday in Huayrurán when I pulled the trigger? Poor Tuset! You should go see him."

"What did you do that for?"

"No reason. I just felt like it. But now it's time to change, don't you think? From now on I'm going to be different. I'm bored of always being the same…. Look, I'm going to paint myself a mole."

"What for?"

"As long as the mole is on my face I'll be a different woman. I promise you you won't recognize me."

"The mole won't last."

"That's possible. It might not even last the morning…."

We went quiet. I couldn't stop looking at Leticia. For the first time I noticed something exquisite, unreal, indefinable in her. I gritted my teeth because I knew if it weren't for that effort I would be capable of coming out with nonsense or breaking into shouts. The emotion must have sent spasms through my lips because Leticia, in turn, started looking at me in a strange way.

"You look," she said, "you look like you're about to cry."

That was what I felt like: a knot of tears in my throat. I would have let them flow if Leticia hadn't noticed. From the middle of the room she admonished me with a finger.

"Take your wails somewhere else. Go on, get out of here. I'm going to get dressed."

I obeyed her without objecting and left on tiptoe as if afraid to break a spell.

Lunch was painful. Lola was lost in thought and could barely swallow a mouthful of food. Felipe, next to her, was doing his best to amuse her, and not managing to do so he started getting impatient. Leonardo was glowering and silent. Ema, from the head of the table, was smiling to herself and seemed to be celebrating a secret victory. Jacinto, in a corner, turned his blank imperturbable face to the vague murmurs of conversation. But it was above all Leticia who was unrecognizable. On her right cheek was a huge mole, and she was attending to Tuset with unusual solicitude. She had eyes only for him and took it upon herself to peel his fruit and fill his glass.

One small detail surprised me. I had noticed that since the day before one of the Huamachuco businessmen kept looking at Tuset. At one point, he couldn't restrain himself, and raising his voice he asked him if he had ever been in Huamachuco.

"No," replied Tuset dryly; and turning toward Leticia he went on with his conversation.

The businessman gazed at him for a while with the stupid expression of a man to whom an absurdity has just been proven.

Toward dusk, Felipe and I were in the bedroom. My uncle's bad mood had gotten worse since lunch. Several times Lola had fled his company to join Jacinto or Leonardo, and in the end she had gone into the living room to play cards with a group of guests. Despite his experience with women, Felipe, who was speedy and didn't play games, had given up and was in a rage, talking about a trip to Trujillo, a vacation in Lima. Just then Jisha came into the room and told him a group of miners was looking for him.

"Damn!" exclaimed Felipe; and pulling on his hat he went out to the patio.

I followed him. Near the back door I saw Parián, Molina, and a dozen other laborers I had met at the mine. They were mostly the oldest ones, the ones who spoke Spanish. Two women were with them. Felipe marched toward them with his chin raised, with his usual look of a man of character. I fell back and stood about twenty steps away, watching him.

When he got to the center of the group, the Indians removed their hats and bowed. Felipe started shouting, raising a clenched fist. His admonitions were getting more and more energetic. Suddenly, in a few seconds, the situation changed. Parián took out a sack from under his poncho and with a nimble movement put it over Felipe's head. Then I saw Felipe fall under a rain of blows.

My first idea was to run to his aid, but fear paralyzed me. Backing away, I rushed to the living room. Leonardo and his friends were chatting, drinking, playing cards.

"Felipe's getting killed!" was all I managed to say.

Leonardo, followed by the most determined, jumped out of the room. Aunt Ema went with him.

"Bolt the gates!" Leonardo shouted to me as he crossed the patio. While I was going to close the main gate I saw Reynaldo, Jacinto, and other people from the hacienda converging from different points to the site of the brawl.

To close the back gate I had to cross the corner of the patio where the fight was going on. It was a confusion of hats, ponchos, and boots, all flying through the air, of screams, of rasping breaths. Some of the Indians were armed with clubs. Reynaldo was brandishing the crossbar from a gate. Out of the corner of my eye I saw Felipe, freed from the sack, his forehead bloodied, crashing his fists into Molina's head while an Indian woman was pulling on him by the neck. When I managed to close the gate the fight was still on. The results were uncertain. Jacinto was fighting tooth and nail with a miner. Aunt Ema was running from one side to the other, landing a blow here, inflicting a scratch there. Leticia, taking shelter under one of the arcades, was biting her fingers, watching the fight, now and then putting a foot forward as if she were getting ready to flee or to join in. The governor of Cachicadán was windmilling his staff around and the blows were deadly. Leonardo had run to the gun-room. One of the businessmen was dragging himself down the hall, bleeding out the nose.

When night fell the fight was decided.

Some of the rebels had given up. Others ran for the gates and were caught with their hands on the bolts and beaten to a pulp. The only one to resist until the end was Parián. As his companions were being led to the dungeon by Tuset and Leonardo, who were carrying guns, he swung around quickly and hit Felipe with a cross. The fight started up again between just those two. Locked in each other's arms, they rolled around the patio; getting up, they fell down again, ran into columns, made doors groan. After one of their numerous rolls, Felipe got up and Parián remained on the ground. He was unconscious. Between two people he was lifted up and taken to the dungeon.

Until midnight Ema and Lola were attending to the injured. The living room looked like a hospital waiting room. All the combatants were bruised except the deaf man, who had joined in only at the end, on the pretext that he hadn't heard the shouting. The only seriously injured one was a Huamachuco businessman who had lost four teeth to a blow from a cudgel. Felipe had a cut on his head, but it was mostly his fists that had suffered. Joking, he said that those Indians sure had hard jaw-bones.

It took a long time for Leonardo's disquiet to abate. He was scared that the rest of the miners were lurking in the area and would wait until dawn to come in through the roof. He calmed down only when an armed group inspected the four roads to the hacienda without seeing a sign of anybody.

He reinforced the bolts on the prison door and kept watch until the next day.

BAD SLEEPERS

All night long, the prisoners were parading into the study to be interrogated. There were thirteen in all, including the women. Most of them were battered and made eloquent signs of repentance. They blamed Parián, saying he had gotten them drunk and tricked them into coming to San Gabriel. The women cried and made revolting scenes. There were very few to express direct complaints that would help explain the cause of the riot. They said the deaf man treated them badly, made them work until after dark, and hadn't let them hold a wake or give their dead companion a decent burial. The deaf man defended himself against these charges and accused the Indians of being drunks, thieves, of having tried to murder him. In the end, he declared he wouldn't go back to the mine and he resigned from his job as foreman.

The result was that work at the mine was suspended. Parián, whose contusions hadn't let him leave the dungeon, and Molina were held. The others were removed from the payroll, even though some of them threw themselves to the ground and begged to keep working. A messenger was sent to the mine to call off work until a new foreman arrived.

I witnessed all these scenes with mixed feelings. During the fight—from which I abstained out of fear, not impartiality—the idea that the rebels might win had terrified me. I could hardly imagine what would have happened then. Leonardo said that we would have all been beheaded. I had keenly desired the triumph of the people from the hacienda, and it was not without wickedness that I watched Parián get knocked down by Felipe's punches. After all, it was the fate of the people I lived with, of those who treated me as one of theirs, that was at stake. It was my own fate and for that reason the outcome relieved me, though I couldn't manage to get excited about it.

It was only later, during the interrogations, when I saw Parián immobilized in the cell with his ribs broken, that I began to doubt the legitimacy of that victory. I didn't approve of that rebellion, but I was able to understand it. There was something desperate, heroic, and at the same time necessary about it. The strangest thing was that it hadn't happened earlier. They Indians were indolent, resigning themselves to their fate, but under the influence of circumstance, where drunkenness and bottled-up anger, the awareness of their destiny, and the instinctive knowledge of their strength came into play, they became bold and were capable of exacting the most ferocious reprisals. Jacinto told me about an uprising three years ago on a neighboring hacienda where the overseer and his family were massacred.

"Every so often something like this happens," he said. "In one place today, somewhere else tomorrow…. Fortunately, they don't all get together because then there wouldn't be one bearded man left around here. But we won't see that happen and our children probably won't either. It's better that way, don't you think? I don't like butchery, no matter how just the motives. I prefer to study engines."

By the third day things were back to normal, and since harvest time was coming, Leonardo decided to go to Angasmarca to recruit labor. He was accompanied by the governor and Tuset, who was heading to Santiago to finish getting ready for his engagement. At the last minute, Leticia decided to join the caravan. Accompanying Tuset for a while was just a pretext, because what she really wanted to do was spend the night in Cachicadán and bathe in the hot springs. The riders left after lunch. Felipe, Lola, and I said goodbye to them at the gate.

That same afternoon, the three of us took a walk to the water mill, which was located on a slope near the house. It was one of the most beautiful places in the hacienda. The water was brought from the lake in a wooden aqueduct held up by tall eucalyptus posts that soared over ravine and road. The old millstone shook with the movement of the wheel and you could hear the noise hundreds of meters away. Inside, it was packed with sacks of wheat and the walls were white with flour.

After the brawl, Lola had ended up accepting Felipe's attentions again, albeit with apparent levity, playing a role that consisted of acting alternately inviting and aloof. The whole walk she did nothing but draw Felipe into gallantry only to scorn it later and provoke advances that she didn't return. Felipe, faced with this frivolous behavior, but at heart rancorous, seemed a little clueless. But when we were returning things changed. Felipe, taking advantage of my inattention, must have undertaken some maneuver, because on the way back he had regained his mastery. Lola, on the other hand, was unsure. Since it was chilly, she let go of Felipe's arm to wrap herself in her shawl. As she went through the gate she mumbled, talking to herself:

"Leonardo and Leticia won't be back until tomorrow. I'll have to spend the night alone."

Felipe didn't answer. I saw him rub his mustache as if protecting his lips from a smile. Reaching the house, he headed resolutely for the living room without even glancing at Lola, who, sighing, sought refuge in her bedroom.

Leonardo's departure didn't change the routine in San Gabriel—that night there was the usual drinking and dancing. Taking advantage of the lack of supervision and believing, besides, to be representing his brother, Jacinto served the guests large glasses of brandy. Back from the walk, I found him quite tipsy and animated by uncommon talkativeness. In general, Leonardo's presence inhibited him, reduced him to the status of a second son, but in his absence he came to the fore and got as much as he could out of the occasion. He gave himself the pleasure of ordering the servants around, disposing freely of the bar, and talking about the problems of the hacienda with the forcefulness of an artful farmer. At first, outsiders listened to him with respect because of the surprising gravity of his facial expression. Besides, he always began his speeches with that irrefutable logic that consists of speaking in clichés. But after some time, as he went on expounding his ideas, there were some lapses in his intelligence and the nonsense began. That night the businessmen listened to him in bafflement, not knowing whether to take him seriously or burst out laughing.

When he saw Felipe he embraced him noisily and brought him into the group.

"I love you a lot!" he exclaimed. "You're the bravest of all! You hit harder than anybody the other day!... And do you remember when you broke Daniel's nose? Gentlemen, nobody can handle Felipe! Once, because of a woman...."

Felipe cut him off. He realized that Jacinto was on the verge of drunkenness.

"You're boring them with those stories. Talk to them instead about your mandolin. Or better yet, play us something."

Jacinto embarked on a discussion about music, but when he saw Felipe's boots he checked himself.

"Have you been at the mill? Surely with Lola. Of course, you and Lola, the two of you, well, I mean that the two of you...."

Felipe gestured with impatience, and to avoid hearing Jacinto's impertinence he approached Ema and asked her to dance. Ema was in a good mood and not even Lola's appearance in the living room—she was wearing a city dress—altered her. On the contrary, when she saw her she cajoled her into coming close and made so bold as to kiss her on the cheek.

"You're a fashion plate. You look like a Lima girl."

I approached the guests. I had spotted the businessman who had asked Tuset once if he was from Huamachuco. His face when he had heard the negative had stayed with me. I started talking to him and soon managed to steer the conversation toward the future couple.

"In a week they'll exchange rings," I told him. "He went to Santiago to get his father, who was appointed mayor."

Only when I asked him if he had met Tuset before did he look at me with distrust.

"I don't know," he told me. "I must be wrong. But I'd swear I've seen him before in Huamachuco. And less than a year ago."

For all my efforts he didn't say another word. Instead, he distanced himself from me, as if my questions discomfited him. I looked for Jacinto, whose voice could no longer be heard. He might have received some confidence about the matter. He was sitting next to the Victrola, staring into the middle of the room with his mouth twisted into a peculiar expression that gave his face the look of a mask of pain. He looked defeated and when I went up to him he paid me no attention. I realized that he was looking at Lola and Felipe, who were dancing on and on. They were playing a pasodoble. Every time the record finished Felipe ran to the machine and started it again. The two of them were spinning dizzily, and their happiness, their nonchalance, increased, by contrast, Jacinto's look of desolation and his anxiety.

"That music, that music," I heard him repeat through his teeth. "It's like a worm in my ear.... That music...."

As Felipe went over to put the record on again Jacinto raised his hand and grabbed him by the wrist. His movement was so quick that it disconcerted Felipe. Since the hand didn't let go of him, he jerked his forearm energetically and got loose. The pasodoble started up again. Then Jacinto got up and with a swipe ran the needle over the record. A horrible screech followed the music and interrupted conversations. The ensuing silence was broken by the sound of a record shattering on the floor.

The imperious gaze with which Felipe turned around distracted me a second, but then it was the look on Jacinto's face that held me. His blue eyes were two steel balls enclosed in red circles. I had seen that look in sick dogs, in great birds of prey.

"To bed!" he shouted, banging the turntable of the Victrola with his fist. "Everybody go to bed! All together, troublemakers, to bed!"

The records started flying. Some flew through the air and hit the walls. Others sailed out the window and landed far away, in the ditches beside the road.

Felipe had rushed over to Jacinto, and grabbing him by his sweater he pushed him against the wall. His head went forward with such momentum I thought he was going to break his nose.

"You drink like a mule when you know you shouldn't even touch a drop! We going to lock you into your room and throw away the key!"

Jacinto lifted his arms, and letting out a shout he gripped Felipe by the neck. The Victrola tottered. The two of them fell to the ground.

Several guests and I rushed over to separate them. They were so firmly locked that at one point I found myself with one of Felipe's boots in my hands. We finally managed to pull them apart. Jacinto was bleating, letting tears fall, and slobbering.

"Aníbal! Aníbal!" he shrieked, struggling in our arms.

Felipe was in a corner rubbing his neck.

"That animal got his nails into me," he said as Ema attended to him.

After a series of incoherent shouts, Jacinto went quiet, his arms hanging limp, his gaze absent.

"Aníbal,..." he sighed, looking at us as if he were searching for a face. "Where's Aníbal?"

"You should take him to his room," suggested Ema.

Jacinto lowered his head into his arms and started crying.

"To the slaughterhouse, to the slaughterhouse,..." he was saying. "You're leading me to the slaughterhouse...."

"He should go to his room," said Felipe, taking a step forward.

"It would be better if you didn't touch him," put in Ema. "Lucho and I will take him."

Jacinto had looked up, and even though the tears kept falling, he was smiling in a way that twisted his mouth painfully toward one ear, as if he had a nervous tic. He kept that same look as Ema and I took him to his room. Ema locked the window and bolted the door as she left.

"Aníbal is his younger brother, the one who died," said Ema as we were going back to the living room. "He fell off a cliff in the days when you traveled to Trujillo on horseback. He was a little crazy and they were taking him to see a doctor."

The gathering broke up in a few minutes. Ema went to bed and the guests did the same after making sure that Jacinto was safely locked away. Lola and Felipe stayed for some time in the living room.

"There's no music left to keep dancing to," observed Felipe, kicking pieces of broken records with his boots.

Lola was pale and didn't dare look up.

"I'm going to bed," she said, leaving the room.

Felipe, his hands in his pockets, went thoughtful. When he noticed me his brow furrowed.

"And you, what are you doing here? You should go to bed."

"I'm not sleepy," I answered.

"You must be in love."

Putting an arm around my neck, he led me to the bedroom.

"It's time to go to bed now," he said. "After a scandal like that there's nothing better than a good night's sleep."

Felipe didn't turn off the light for a long time. For a long time I heard him moving around in bed. I hadn't heard his boots fall, so I imagined he was still dressed. His insomnia was contagious, and Jacinto couldn't have been sleeping either, because the sound of his footsteps carried through the wall. The flicker of a match let me know Felipe was smoking. Several other matches followed. As I had made a slight noise, I heard him say to me:

"Are you awake?"

I didn't answer him and I went still under the covers. The minutes went by with atrocious slowness. Half an hour later I heard him get up and open the bedroom door. A gust of cold air hit my face. The door closed.

I jumped out of bed right away. My vigil was justified: I had sensed Felipe would leave. On the way back from the mill, Lola had been clear about her nighttime solitude, uttering words that were almost an invitation.

Barefoot, I slid out into the hall. In the shadows I saw Felipe's silhouette advancing cautiously. The door to Lola's room was the third off the cloister leading to the kitchen. A fringe of light showed through the cracks.

Lola wasn't sleeping either. But to my great surprise, Felipe went on by without even pausing and disappeared into the depths of the hallway leading to the inner rooms. Quickening my pace, I tried to gain ground so that my curiosity could absorb even the dregs of this act of espionage. All at once, a shadow arose so abruptly that I couldn't suppress a yell. It was Alfredo, who, in pajamas like me, stood in my way.

"Where are you going?" he muttered, raising an arm. "What are you looking for? Go on, get out of here!"

His actions were so firm that to advance I would have had to fight him. Without a word I turned around and went back to my bedroom.

For a while I remained awake listening to Jacinto's footsteps, but thinking about Felipe's destination. I realized then that a fifth person must have been awake, with the tenacious wakefulness of someone who is waiting. And that fifth person had to be Aunt Ema.

A Fugitive

*L*eonardo came back radiant from Angasmarca. He had managed to recruit one hundred-twenty day laborers, so he was assured of enough people to bring in his harvest. He had also been told that it had been raining for two days in Otuzco, and the sky in San Gabriel was already starting to cloud over. These events improved the outlook for the hacienda and made it possible to look forward to the future with optimism.

But soon after his return he heard the bad news about Jacinto's condition. Felipe gave him a brief summary of the incident in a comic way, trying to absolve himself of all responsibility.

"He was as drunk as a horse. We had to shut him up in his room."

Leonardo said nothing, but it was obvious that the news bothered him. Later, as I walked by his study, I heard him calling me. He was alone, rustling through a stack of papers.

"I want to talk to you," he said, without interrupting his work. "I've been thinking you might be useful to me in the hacienda. Since Daniel left I haven't had an accountant. Do you want to be in charge of the harvest accounts? There are thousands of documents I need to put in order. Naturally, I'll pay you a salary. What I owe you from the mine will be added on. Right now I don't have any money."

I heard out his offer without much enthusiasm. I would have preferred, in any case, a job outside where I could get to know the land. Despite my long stay in San Gabriel, I was still a city dweller lost in the pastures who couldn't tell the difference between barley and wheat and who saw only countryside where everybody else recognized the metamorphosis of a maternal force.

"If you do a good job," he added, "you might be able to keep the job permanently. After all, you're one of ours, and I need to start thinking about your future."

I don't know why that statement of his bothered me. My logical reaction would have been to rejoice, since a large measure of my anxiety stemmed from my inactivity and my idleness. But maybe the very fact of his disposing of my future irritated me. My future was my only treasure, and I respected it to such an extreme that I never dared profane it with any important plans. Only the few times that I was blinded by passion did I make crude use of it and become capable of consuming it in the instant of a dream. But my natural attitude was usually one of waiting. I considered it a virtue that let me recognize in each favorable event a legacy of destiny.

Leonardo had gone quiet too, his gazed fixed lifelessly on his papers. When he went introspective, he seemed to plunge a hundred fathoms below life, and the only part of him remaining on the surface, like the funnel of a sinking ship, was the smoking tip of his cigarette.

"I worry about a lot of things," he said at last. "Jacinto, for example. Why do they let him drink so much. He's not aggressive, he's incapable of attacking anybody…. I don't understand it! You were there when it happened?"

I told him what I had seen. When I mentioned the name Aníbal he smiled somewhat sadly.

"Aníbal always defended him when we kids fought," he explained. "The two of them were always together; they understood each other without exchanging a word. My mother and Aníbal died around the same time. That was terrible. Jacinto's had something wrong with him since then. Jacinto is very sensitive. What I don't understand is what he's got against Felipe."

"Could it be because of Lola?" I suggested.

"What's Lola got to do with it?"

"Lola looks like the pictures…. She looks like his mother."

"You noticed it too?" His gaze looked me over distrustfully. "I ought to tell you something: in reality, those are pictures of Lola, not our mother. Jacinto took them out of my photo album and got everything mixed up."

I still hadn't reacted to that revelation when Leonardo added:

"That woman will have to be sent back to her farm as soon as possible. Let's go see Jacinto."

The room was in shadow. When Leonardo opened the window we saw Jacinto barefoot, in pajamas, squatting next to the bed. He immediately got up and put his face to the wall. As long as we were in the room he stayed that way and only now and then did he turn his head to look at us out of the corner of his eye. It was strange: his beard had grown quickly, as if nourished by sorrow or suffering.

"Let's go," ordered Leonardo.

We walked silently through the cloister.

"I'm afraid he'll have to go back to the asylum," murmured Leonardo, who disappeared into the inner rooms.

I stayed under the arcades watching dusk fall. Zarco, Colla, and the other hacienda dogs were running back and forth over the patio keeping watch over the flight of the hawks. I thought about Jacinto, about his oppressive and sad fate. His loneliness seemed horrible to me; horrible as well his lack of a woman; but even worse the calamity of dying without progeny. I told myself that a child was sometimes all it took to restore meaning and greatness to the most pointless life. But Jacinto showed all the signs of being the last of a breed, one of those attempts where the human race goes astray and dies out.

That thought made me shudder. I felt the need to seek out the others, to take refuge in the shade of a conversation. My loneliness was beginning to seem to me like a sickness or an ill omen. I was just about to get up when I saw Leticia leaning on a column a few steps away. Her appearances were always unpredictable. I was convinced that she emerged from the wind, had made a pact with objects.

"What are you thinking about," she asked. "You've been staring at the clouds for a while. You shouldn't look at the clouds or the moon too much or you'll go crazy."

I shifted my gaze back to the patio. The dogs were wallowing in the dust.

"I'm thinking that Jacinto won't have children."

"Always thinking strange things, when there are such happy things to think about."

She took a few steps and sat down next to me. Her eyes examined the sky.

"It's going to rain."

I looked at her. Her face, in the evening light, had a pearly pallor, seemed to be made, like wax masks, of a translucent material. But instead of a sickly pallor like Alfredo's it was a pallor of privilege: the pallor of a life contained and punished by the delicacy of form. Only the mole on her cheek added a mundane touch.

"You must not have washed your face in the baths at Cachicadán," I whispered.

"Why? I was in the pool for half an hour and I got out only because I was about to faint."

"The mole still hasn't worn off."

Leticia grabbed her cheek and smiled.

"What a fool you are! I paint it back on every morning."

"It'll never disappear that way."

"One of these days I'll forget."

I stopped talking. It was still getting dark. The first raindrops raised dust.

"Do you want it to disappear?"

I looked at her again. There was no malice in her question. For the last few days, sweetness, serenity, had dominated her behavior.

"I wish it would never disappear," I answered. "You've kept your promise to change and now you're different. I feel as if you've grown away from me, but I don't mind. You're better this way and that's enough."

Leticia became lost in thought. Bringing her legs in out of the rain, she intertwined her fingers around her knees. In the dark, her profile went blurry.

"And I'm going to tell you something else. I'm going to tell you that it bothered me before that you were getting engaged, but now that's what I want you to do, I really do. It would be very sad if you got to be Lola's age and still weren't married, not knowing what to do with your life, with your hands, with anything."

"It's what I want too," said Leticia. "Look: I'll have an amazing wedding dress. The train will be so long that all the maids together won't be enough to carry it. The church will have to be full of flowers and there will be lots of candles. If I have twelve sons I'll name them after the apostles. If I have fourteen, after the Incas. But why so many? Three would be enough. They'll be the three wise men!"

She laughed hard when she said that. Before the echo brought her voice back to her, she had gone quiet. The silence was prolonged. When I looked in her direction I could see only profound darkness. I put my hand out boldly, sure that she wasn't there anymore, that I would touch only an emptiness that would hurt me. Against my expectations, I felt the shape of her arm. Leticia, instead of protesting, took my hand in hers and lay it on her lap.

"Why are you trembling?" she asked. With her thin fingertips she caressed my fingers. "You have a small hand. A woman's hand. It's almost like mine. Have you seen my Dad's hands, or Tuset's? They're big red hands full of hair. They're hands that have worked. But yours look like you've kept them hidden and were saving them for something or other."

Those words, spoken in a distracted tone that almost made them indifferent, moved me deeply. I would have liked to hug her out of a dark feeling made up mostly of gratitude, but I was afraid the gesture would be interpreted as a low requital of love.

"Leonardo told me that if I want I can stay at the hacienda working as the accountant," I mumbled. "I haven't answered him yet, but I think I'll accept."

Leticia let my hand drop heavily and remained quiet. The first flash of lightning freed the outline of the hills from the darkness.

"Let's go," she said, standing up. "We could've been struck by that bolt, same as Pauca last year, the shepherd. What would they have thought if they found us dead holding hands? My feet are wet."

As I was getting up, footsteps sounded in the hall. Soon a shadow appeared. For a while it circled us irresolutely. We recognized Lola.

"Is it you? Where's the hall light?"

Groping in the dark, I turned it on. Lola was wrapped in her shawl, her eyelids red, her face pained.

"Why do they want me to leave San Gabriel?" she asked. "Is it that I bother them too much? I just got through talking to Aunt Ema and my father and they say I have to leave after the ceremony Saturday."

Just then, clearly, we heard hoofbeats on the road.

"How strange!" said Leticia. "Sounds like somebody's coming late to the hacienda."

"I barely have a month," said Lola, "and they won't even let me stay for the harvest."

I tried to console her but I couldn't find the right words. I was thinking that Leonardo hadn't taken too long about getting to work on his worries. Leticia and Lola stayed quiet, as if each were inhibited by the other.

"What are we doing here?" asked Lola. "It's cold. Let's go to the living room."

The three of us started walking.

"I couldn't get to sleep last night," continued Lola. "Someone was walking along the hall. Who could it have been?"

"It could have been the ghosts," replied Leticia absently as we entered the living room.

The guests had departed and there were only family members. Leonardo and Felipe were standing next to the window and talking. I thought I heard them talking about Jacinto. Everything indicated that Leonardo was determined to resolve in the most peremptory fashion all the internal problems of the hacienda. Felipe was assenting, his glass in hand, irony visible in the corners of his mustache. The poise with which he tolerated Leonardo's presence was admirable. At one point he slapped him on the back with such naturalness that I was assailed by doubts and wondered if his nocturnal outing hadn't had another goal. Why would it have to be Aunt Ema? They only one who might know was Alfredo. I was beginning to understand his shifty behavior, his fits of anger, his sufferings. I would have to wait until dinner to approach him.

Aunt Ema was in a corner knitting. There was nothing to be read in her expression either. The only thing I noticed was that she looked insistently at Leticia and me, one after the other. Did she suspect something? I knew she was sharp, intuitive. Just in case, I walked away from Leticia, who, since we had entered the living room, had remained wordless by my side.

In vain did I look for Alfredo at dinner; his seat was empty. Nobody else seemed to notice. It was only halfway through the meal that Leonardo asked about him.

"He must be eating in the kitchen," answered Ema.

Jisha, who was coming in with the dishes, was questioned and responded in the negative. Someone suggested that he was playing out in the country and was coming back late. We finished dinner and there was no sign of him.

Until ten we were in the living room, waiting. Jisha, accompanied by Zarco, had gone to look outside, a lantern in his hand. His search was fruitless. Worried, Leonardo ordered the hacienda gates left open. Ema had sunk into her armchair, an absent look in her eyes. Felipe was smoking, looking out the window.

That was when Ollanta, who as usual was mutely and indifferently witnessing all our problems, spoke up.

"He must have gone to Santiago," he said.

Leonardo looked at him in bafflement.

"Or Trujillo," added Ollanta. "He's been wanting to go for a while."

"What are you saying?" asked Leonardo, moving toward him.

"He must be talking nonsense," put in Aunt Ema.

"Keep on!" Leonardo ordered him.

Ollanta, seeing the sudden importance he was accorded, was perturbed.

"I don't know!" he exclaimed. "I don't know anything. All I know is that at six he left his room with a bag and I haven't seen him since."

Leonardo threw a poncho over his shoulders and left the living room.

"Odd," muttered Felipe, throwing his cigarette butt on the floor.

"To Santiago!" repeated Ema quietly.

The six of us said nothing. We heard the rain drumming on the roof. A cold war of gazes ensued. Eyes turned like lanterns, met in midair, and after a brief skirmish took different paths. A kind of inexplicable shame weighed us down.

Leonardo showed up out of breath.

"Chicuelo isn't in the stable! How the hell did it occur to him to take my horse? With yesterday's ride from Cachicadán he's exhausted. I'll have to go and get him."

"We heard a rider go by around dusk," murmured Leticia pensively.

"Are you going to go?" asked Ema, who was suddenly prey to keen animation. "You're very tired…. Let Felipe go instead."

"Yes," put in Felipe. "Give me the mare Flor and I'll catch up with him before he gets to the bridge and bring him back by the ears."

"This is my business," answered Leonardo. "Go to Mollepata instead and have a telegram sent to Mabila in Santiago. We've got to be ready for anything. And everybody else go to bed! I might not be able to make it back until tomorrow."

The two horsemen galloped away in opposite directions. Disobeying Leonardo, the rest of us sat in the living room. There was no point trying to start a conversation. Everyone seemed to be pondering his own affairs. Ema had lit a cigarette—something unusual for her—and was blowing smoke out her nose.

"Who could have been walking up and down the hall last night?" asked Lola.

As an answer, Leticia stood up, smiled, stretched, and left the living room without saying goodnight.

When I went to bed only Ema and Lola were left, each sitting at one end of the sofa, not looking at each other, separated by a silence full of foreboding.

PREPARATIONS

*T*he nearness of the engagement ceremony changed the way San Gabriel looked. All the hacienda people were mobilized for the preparations for the party. A room to receive the fiancé and his father in had been fixed up. The living room wallpaper, whose colors were faded, had been replaced and the rugs were beaten on the patio with branches from orange trees. A *pachamanca* specialist was contracted and Felipe went to Pallasca just to hire a group of musicians.

The strangest event of those four days was the return of Leonardo and Alfredo. I spent the night of the escape worried, sensing that some scandal was about to break. The next day I woke up early and noticed that Felipe hadn't gone to bed. Getting dressed quickly, I went to the living room. Aunt Ema was still sitting on the sofa, her face worn out by the vigil, a pile of cigarette butts in the ashtray. Felipe, whose head was sunk into his chest, had fallen asleep in an armchair. Later he woke up and went to his bedroom. Soon afterward he reappeared clean-shaven, washed, a cigarette hanging from his lips, and to hide his unease he started walking under the arcades.

It was only after breakfast that we heard the trot of the horses. Leonardo and Alfredo appeared on the patio. The two of them, their faces covered with road dust, were smiling. Leonardo dismounted and came over to us.

"That boy made me run a good race! I caught up with him past the bridge. Don't get mad at him, because I already read him the riot act! It's all our fault. The kid's bored here and he needs to spend some time in Trujillo. We've already discussed it."

Alfredo nodded. But his assent seemed to me slightly feigned. He turned his back to us and went to his room.

"Okay!" added Leonard when he saw Ema and Felipe looking at him in disbelief. "That's taken care of. Let's not waste a minute. There's a lot of work to do." And without adding another word he walked away from the group to shut himself in his study.

Disconcerted, Felipe and Ema remained there looking at each other. When the study door closed, Ema shrugged her shoulders as a sign of her indifference or astonishment. Felipe blew out a slow mouthful of smoke and went to the living room, where he poured himself a huge glass of pisco.

From then on I busied myself observing Leonardo. Nothing in his temperament seemed to have changed unless it was his sudden and almost obsessive passion for work. He did nothing but add and subtract figures, order around Tacuri—he was the foreman—supervise the renovation of the house, and gallop as often as twice a day to the cultivated fields. Mornings, he was the first up and evenings, after dinner, he gulped his coffee down to take refuge in his study and resume his solitary toil. The result of this policy was that he didn't have time to talk to anybody, and when he did, at meals, he did so outwardly, as if he were swallowing the juice of his answers and letting out only the chewed-up words.

It occurred to me again that Alfredo had to know something. After his thwarted flight, he had rejoined the life of the family with apparent docility, but deep down he was still a loner who accepted caresses without the slightest grace and took advantage of the first opportunity to flee from groups of people. I was lying in wait for the chance to interview him, and it presented itself on one of his usual excursions to the eucalyptus grove.

On the edge of the grove there was a small hollow where wild blackberries grew over the damp grass. When I got there, Alfredo was leaning over putting the berries into the crown of his hat. Sitting down next to him, I talked to him about trivial things as I waited for the right moment.

"Alfredo!" I said at last. "I'm not going to ask you why you tried to run away the other night—"

"And I'm not going to tell you either!" he interrupted me sharply.

"You don't need to tell me. The only thing I want to know is what you talked about with Leonardo. I thought he was going to punish you, that he was going to beat you, but you both came back all smiles, as if you'd been on vacation."

Alfredo went pensive, his fragile nose dilating as he breathed.

"You want to know everything!" he answered. "You're a spy like Ollanta. You're always watching other people. What were you doing the other night in the hall?"

"I was following Felipe."

Alfredo got up. He had gone paler.

"Felipe was going to the kitchen to make himself a coffee!"

"I believe you. I'm not interested in that."

Alfredo sat down again.

"To make himself a coffee," he repeated under his breath.

It wasn't the moment to press him. Alfredo, gazing out over the Huayrurán hills as his fingers distractedly squeezed the blackberries, had gone quiet. The silence around us grew until it became intolerable.

I had counted the song of a dove in the nearby grove four times.

"I haven't told Leonardo anything," he finally began. "He hasn't asked me anything either. When he caught up with me past the bridge, I got scared and jumped off the horse to hide behind an adobe wall. But he only came up to me and gave me a big hug. 'Let's go back. We'll talk on the way,' he said to me. And we went back."

"What did you talk about?"

"He told me he was going to send me next month to Trujillo or Chiclayo, where there's a big school. He also said that when I came back to San Gabriel on holiday everything would be different, everything a lot prettier, the way it was a long time ago."

"And about the money?"

"What money?"

"Don't play the innocent. The money you took from his study once. How were you going to live once you'd run away? You had a whole plan worked out."

"I'll give it back to him."

As he said that he got up and stood gazing attentively at the roof of the house, as if signaling me that our talk was over.

"Aren't you coming back?"

"I'm going to stay here a while," he answered, and holding out his hands stained by the juice of the blackberries, he said: "Look, it looks like I flayed a lamb."

When I got to the grove I looked back. He was still standing there contemplating his hands with a kind of pained fascination.

The kitchen was the part of the house where, in the days prior to the engagement, activity was concentrated. Drawn toward that room, as if by centrifugal force, were all the inhabitants of San Gabriel. I myself experienced that magnetism and spent hours next to the kitchen range watching the women at work. The cooks—two fat Indian women who looked like twins—rolled from one side of the room to the other, plucking a chicken, stirring a vat full of blancmange. Ema, Lola, and Leticia were dedicated to the making of nougats, meat pies, pastries, and a thousand kinds of sweets, foods whose recipes they kept secret. Felipe turned up now and then to drink a glass of chicha next to the stove or to gnaw on a piece of chicken. The guinea pigs ran around underfoot in alarm, doubtless sensing one of those celebrations that decimated their colony. The fattest ones hardly dared peek out the door to their caves made of adobe bricks. In the shadows you could see their red pupils shining.

My role was merely that of an obliging spectator who seemed to take calm pleasure in the contemplation of other people's work. Only on a very few occasions, when it was a matter of some mechanical task, was my aid sought. I felt good there; I was beginning to understand the majesty of provincial kitchens in the domain of myth, their packed-earth floors, their heavy smells, the crackle of the fire in the heavy stoves. Besides, my curiosity found fertile terrain for observation there. The three women were at my mercy, and their distraction as they worked with their hands seemed to suppress censorship, because their faces reflected their subtlest states of mind with admirable fidelity. The three of them usually kept quiet, and the surprising thing was that, even though they often had their hands in the same dough, their minds were a long way away and each of the women was living at her own secret rhythm. I had fun comparing Lola and Aunt Ema, setting them up against each other like two rivals, and that comparison let me spot features that observing the two women in isolation would have kept from me. Felipe's preference sometimes seemed to me incomprehensible. It's true that Lola, apart from her sad eyes, veiled by thick eyelashes, had no other beautiful feature, but she had a robust body and her health was her most precious attribute. In the last few days she had had another attack, but nobody took them seriously anymore, attributing them to an excess of vitality, not to a defect. Ema, on the other hand, was small, agile, restless. She was well past thirty and her face already seemed to fear the noon sun. But when shadows blurred her features, you could see a certain temperament, a certain inner strength that was powerfully attractive. In addition, her body, which I tried to picture under her outfit, still had some flexibility, and her flesh that odd softness presaging the twilight of sex. When Felipe came in—always with his slightly forced aplomb— Ema seemed not to notice him or, at most, she addressed him with indifference. Lola, on the other hand, didn't say a word, her big eyes kept him in sight, and when he disappeared she would gaze for a long time at the doorway.

Leticia, next to her mother and sister, seemed like a being of another species. The tenacious attention she paid to her work sharpened her features. I was sure she was surrounded by an atmosphere that protected her from all contaminants. It was a real atmosphere, a kind of bodily emanation that allowed me to sense her presence in a room before I crossed the threshold or that revealed her passage through a place she had gone through slightly earlier. Maybe that was why even when you were near her she seemed to keep a certain distance, and in the confusion of a group, impregnable solitude. The activity of the last few days had exhausted her and her pallor had taken on an almost luminous force that emphasized the darkness of her eyes and the outline of her mole. Of the three women, she was the only one to talk, always in a absent-minded tone, not worrying about getting an answer, as if she were obeying a need to be expansive. That's why her subsequent silences seemed more serious and somehow impregnated with mute suffering. I intuited that she was hiding at great cost a secret state of nervous excitement. Her hands, above all, which worked with desperate speed, seemed to give off sparks whenever they touched anything.

My presentiments were confirmed when, one afternoon, we received an unexpected visit in the kitchen. All at once, Jacinto appeared in the doorway. He was wearing a carelessly tied bathrobe that showed his hairy legs. His unshaven face, his gaze of a superhuman brightness, and that smile between ironic and tragic rending his lips made him truly terrifying.

When she saw him, Leticia let out a shout that took my breath away. It was a shout that had been delivered with her whole body, leaving her drained, her hands stilled, her lips colorless. Meanwhile, Jacinto, after kicking the guinea pigs around, knocking down a chair, rushed over to the vat of blancmange and at the risk of getting them skinned put his hands in it. Right away, as the uproar was reaching its climax, Ema ran to get Leonardo. Only after Leonardo and Felipe between them dragged Jacinto out of the kitchen did Leticia react with a fit of anger at herself.

"What an idiot I am! I was so absorbed! It's not as if I'd seen the devil."

Soon afterward she recovered her calm and even tried to exaggerate it by trying out a few jokes. But her voice betrayed her, and when I looked at her I could see huge circles around her eyes, where fear seemed entrenched.

The eve of the engagement, the activity in the hacienda degenerated into tumult. The musicians had come from Pallasca and a large procession from Santiago. Tuset came with his father and his older brother. Also there were Don Evaristo and his wife, who, when they heard about the engagement, put forward the date of their journey to the interior so they could participate in the celebration. Aunt Mabila and the Santiago police chief rounded off the group. The latter's participation was completely accidental. He had mounted his horse drunk and had joined the procession without knowing what it was about and naturally without having been invited. When they got to the pampas he suffered a fall that knocked lucidity back into him. But by then he was too close to San Gabriel to give up on the adventure. With a battered leg he was cussing in the living room and, along with Felipe, starting to savor the first shots of pisco.

Leonardo had to abandon his work to mix with his guests. Surrounded by them, he was masterful in his old role as the host, though he couldn't manage to conceal an unease that he imputed to fatigue. That same afternoon, during a brief escape to the study to finish off some accounts, he had an unrestrainable fit of anger.

"I'm sick of seeing so many people!" he shouted. "The whole time talking with some, smiling at others! As if I didn't have anything else to do. Jacinto keeps getting worse; he broke his mandolin and threw a bunch of junk out the window. Harvest time's coming and I still haven't worked out the payroll. Good thing there will only be three of us at the hacienda next month."

Those last words made me think. Who might those three people be? When I asked him what he meant he looked at me impatiently.

"It's a manner of speaking! Three, four, or five, it's all the same. But not twenty!"

His response didn't satisfy me. I was troubled the rest of the evening. In the living room, Leticia, dressed up as if for a party, was attending to her future father-in-law with an exquisite amiability that annoyed me. From the start Tuset's father looked repugnant to me. He was a man in his sixties whose Slavic origin was revealed only by his last name and the reddish color of his jowls. His fatness was an affront, and to accommodate his stomach he had to sit on the edge of his chair with his legs spread wide. His appointment as mayor—a reward for twenty years of absurd scheming—had made him tiresome and solemn. He spoke with expansive gestures about the problems facing the town, called the council members animals, and bragged about giving eleven jerseys to the city soccer team. His son's alliance with Leticia, although he would never admit it, made him swell with pride. Though his solid fortune needed no prop, he couldn't stop thinking of himself, at heart, as a rich salesman, so being related to Leonardo, a small farmer, let him bathe in that aureole of aristocracy always given off by the possession of land.

After dinner, Leticia, who had behaved until then with admirable refinement, started showing signs of fatigue. Several times I saw her repress a sigh under her napkin or become lost in thought, her cheek resting in her hand, in an attitude of complete surrender. In the end she got Leonardo's permission to go rest.

Half an hour later I went out to the cloister. The guests' talk had become tedious. I was walking in front of Leticia's room with the vague hope that she would come out. I felt like talking to her, telling her, though I didn't know why, that I was with her. In the end I couldn't wait any longer and I put my ear to the door. There was the sound of sobbing that was cut off now and then only to start up again with greater suffering. That discovery upset me and I rapped furiously on the door with my knuckles. Silence followed. Then a shutter opened slightly and out came the oval of Leticia's face, eyes red, cheeks wet.

"I knew it was you," she said to me dryly. "What do you want?"

"I don't know. I thought you were feeling bad. I thought you might need something."

"Yes, I do. I need you to get me a cigarette."

"What for?" I asked stupidly.

"What do you think. Run! You might get caught wandering around here."

I ran to Felipe's room and took a cigarette from his night table. After taking it, Leticia slammed the door with such force that it just about crushed my fingers. It was only as I was going back to my room that I realized it: the mole had disappeared from Leticia's cheek.

THE ACT

*B*reakfast was served at ten-thirty with great solemnity. Besides the ham, there were platters with pieces of chicken, wedges of fresh cheese, sponge cakes, honey. Tuset, who had been wearing his blue Sunday suit since eight in the morning, was going from one side to another telling nonsensical jokes that he alone laughed at. Out of the corner of his eye, he kept a close watch on the dining room door, waiting for Leticia's entrance. It was futile; Leticia didn't show up.

Lola got to the table late. She was worried, and when somebody asked her about Leticia she said she was a bit tired and would get up in time for lunch. After breakfast she took Leonardo by the arm and guided him into a corner. They whispered together for a few minutes. At last, Leonardo, his face puffy, left the living room and headed resolutely to Leticia's room.

Ten minutes later he was back. With a sign to Aunt Ema, he went to the study. Felipe, who, even though he was chatting with Don Evaristo, hadn't stopped observing the scene, followed them. Lola and I brought up the rear.

When the five of us were in the study, Leonardo closed the door.

"It's like this," he said. "That crazy Leticia doesn't want to get out of bed. She says she doesn't want to see anybody and that Tuset, his family, and the musicians can go take their music somewhere else."

After a brief shock, Ema started shouting to high heaven and tried to rush into Leticia's room ready to use persuasion or force.

"Wait!" ordered Leonardo. "We can't work things out that way. We've got to take things calmly. In the first place we have to wait for that girl to calm down."

"But what does she plan to do?"

"That's what I don't know yet. But I do know I'm not going to allow that girl to play games with us. I'm sick of her whims."

Ema supported her husband's arguments. With her usual inspiration for vitriol, she let loose a barrage of insults against Leticia.

"Has she gotten dressed? Waiting until the last minute, the stupid girl! She could have said something earlier. We've even got the priest in to bless the rings!"

"The truth is," sighed Leonardo, "that deep down none of this matters to me. Whether she gets engaged or not, whether she gets married or stays single, is all the same to me. The only thing that kills me is looking bad in front of everybody. You can't just go tell Tuset and his father: 'Go home. My daughter changed her mind.' People will be jab-bering about it for a whole year!... And the mine? What are we going to do about the mine? We still haven't made it over. That business will go to hell!"

The debate continued for the rest of the morning. Leonardo got angrier and angrier. At last, Felipe, who hadn't said anything, spoke up.

"I think this is all your fault. You only need eyes in your head to see that Leticia was never interested in Tuset and all she's done is have fun at his expense."

Leonardo didn't know what to say.

"Maybe," he said finally. "But I don't have time to start studying other people's thoughts. If things happen behind my back, so much the worse."

Those words seemed to carry a depth charge. Felipe, slightly tremu-lous, went quiet.

"Leticia has been putting on an act," he dared to answer.

"Let her act it out until the end!"

The meeting broke up. Leonardo and Ema went to Leticia's room to make her get up. Felipe went back to the living room. Lola and I stayed on the patio.

We sat there for a long time without saying anything, letting the sun toast us. Lola had put an arm around my neck and I felt her forehead resting on my shoulder. Looking at her up close, I saw a fine down over her lip. She was mouthing a song. Days earlier, Leticia had sat next to me in that same place, my hand in hers. The situation was repeating itself, but one of the terms of the equation had changed, That may have been why I observed Lola without shaking and, like a pedestal, sup-ported that weight coldly.

"Let's go see Leticia," she said to me suddenly. "Leonardo and Ema must be finished now."

In effect, the two of them were coming out talking and heading back to the living room. We ran across the patio.

Leticia, in a nightgown, was standing in front of the mirror brush-ing her hair. In her slightly altered features, in her bright eyes, there were still traces of irritation. But her movements were slow, seemingly expressive of serene conformity.

"So you're up!" sighed Lola.

"Why not? After all, the afternoon should be a lot of fun. There'll even be a speech! I've heard my father-in-law has one prepared."

"And what will you do later?"

"Later?" Leticia left her brush on the dressing table and went pensive. With her arms crossed she took a few steps around the room. "I don't know what I'll do. Put the ring in an envelope and give it back to him."

I stood up. I was really troubled. It wasn't just Leticia's words. The sunlight penetrated the sheer cloth of her nightgown, outlining her thighs with such clarity that I nearly had the feeling of physical contact. Sweat began to roll down my forehead. I thought immediately about the river.

"I'm going to go for a swim," I said. "It's really hot."

"If you're going to the river I'll go with you," put in Lola. "This Leticia has given me such a headache with her problems. I need to cool off."

"You're leaving," murmured Leticia with an odd inflection, turning her back on us.

I went to the bedroom to get my swimsuit. Lola's decision to come along discomfited me. I would rather have gone alone. In my conscience I sensed a massing of confusing feelings that I needed to analyze calmly.

At the back gate I ran into Lola in a huge straw hat that made her look slightly ridiculous. We walked without a word down the path to the river. For me, that path was full of memories. I recognized the tree, then the bend where I tripped and fell. In the background, between trees and the sound of running water, was the riverbank.

Lola, her somber face lowered, had a little trouble walking. Now and then she looked up to take in the landscape and sigh. Sweat was pouring down her temples.

"I've got to go tomorrow," she murmured at last. "Don Evaristo is traveling to the interior and my father wants me to go with him."

"Too bad," I answered, but I realized right away my phrase lacked conviction, that it had rolled off my tongue like words of condolence at a wake. "Who do you live with there?" I added, trying to show a certain interest.

"With my mother. Just the two of us. Nobody else."

When I looked at her I saw her cheeks flushed, suffering in their magnificent maturity. I felt sorry for her.

"And do you never get visitors?" I continued.

"No, never."

We reached the riverbank just then. The current wound joyfully among the rocks, throwing up a white spray that the sun struck and made iridescent. In the shallows you could see to the bottom, where moss grew and pebbles gleamed. In a bend my cousins had built a dam so that the water would back up and form a kind of artificial pool. The water there went up to the neck of an adult and it was possible to swim a few strokes.

Lola went into the bushes and I took advantage of her absence to put on my swimsuit. Then I sank into the cool current. Floating on my back, I could see the rough mass of the hill of the cross covered with its thorny vegetation. Along its narrow paths traveled a few stray goats. Against the deep sky flew by now and then flocks of white doves, yellow woodpeckers, red-breasted linnets. The landscape here had a concrete beauty. You could distinguish the shapes, colors, and edges of things. It wasn't like the coast, where the ocean, the dunes, and the fogs created a thousand mirages and impregnated everything with vagueness and melancholy.

Lola came into the pool. I realized it only when she started splashing by my side. Putting her head in, she let her thick black mane get wet and then threw it back energetically. We started turning around each other like two fish in a fishbowl. Our movements had a strange gravity, becoming harmonious at times, ritualistic, as if we were acting out an allegory. Once or twice we took each other by the hand and sank until we touched the rocks with our chests. When we came up we would laugh out loud and our laughter, like music, pleased us. At one point our bodies touched underwater and I felt on my leg the sudden warm weight of a naked thigh. With powerful strokes, I swam immediately away. The water started to feel cold. A little while later I got out and lay down on the rocks, protecting myself from the sun with my shaking fingers.

From that strange perspective, I saw Lola emerge from the pool. I realized then that she didn't have a swimsuit, only a simple petticoat that the water made cling to her body. Picking it up by the edge she shook it over her thighs, sending thousands of luminous drops into the air. Then I saw her legs, her knees, and at last her feet approaching me. Spreading out a big towel, she lay down on her back.

I closed my eyes. Without seeing Lola, I sensed her presence; I pictured the fullness of her body. There was nothing but the burning sun and a silence that I felt myself falling into as if into an abyss. In the end, I couldn't take it anymore and, energetically, I propped my head on my elbow.

Lola had closed her eyes too and covered her body with the towel. That precaution humiliated me and I decided to retreat. As I was getting up, Lola's lips parted.

"I must have gotten too much exercise," she sighed. "My ears are buzzing, my chest is starting to hurt."

I stayed still, not knowing what to say.

"Give me your hand," she added. "You're going to have to give me a massage."

I held my hand out cautiously and Lola, pulling off the towel, uncovered a large white breast furrowed with small blue veins. Grabbing my hand, she put it on her breast, smoothly at first, then stronger, finally frenetically. I felt the flesh harden and palpitate under my hand. At last, with an abrupt movement, she pushed aside my hand and lay there lifeless, her arms limp, her knees trembling. I was keenly curious about her expression, and for a second I thought she was suffering a violent illness. But right then she sat up, opened her eyes for the first time, and looked at me as if she didn't know me. Her pupils seemed to have gone liquid.

"Let's go!" she exclaimed. "Lunch is almost ready!"

I followed her up the path, a few steps behind, silent, stupefied, tripping over rocks as if I were drunk.

Only the sight of Leticia managed to pull me out of my confusion. She was dressed in white, a gold cross on her breast, a crown of orange blossoms in her hair. There wasn't a trace of make-up on her face, giving her such a look of purity that it almost hurt. Her manner was resigned, sweet, at times exasperatingly slow. Sitting in a corner of the patio, under a yellow sun that enveloped her in an irresistible glow, she had her fingers in Tuset's big, coarse hands. The two of them were somewhat separated from the rest of the group, as if they were a decorative set, and they were talking in confidential tones that softened the hearts of the older people and induced you to philosophize about love.

The other guests were spread out around the big castle of rocks built by the *pachamanca* specialist. Chairs, benches, little tables, carpets had been brought out, and the whole set-up looked grotesque at times, as if a drawing room had been improvised in the middle of the wilderness. The atmosphere was festive: you could hear laughter, clapping, corks popping out of bottles, and even Leonardo and Ema had cloaked their bad moods of the morning with ceremonial dress and bonhomie.

All the hacienda servants—taking advantage of the democratic climate created by great festivities—were participating in the chatter, and circulating among the guests were the Negro Reynaldo, the carpenter Tobías, Tacuri, Jisha, and their respective families. The musicians, with their scarlet cummerbunds and big felt fats, were drinking chicha and tuning their instruments. The smell of the beans, tamales, and cooking meat stimulated the appetite and promised a memorable feast.

I wandered for a while from one cluster to another, not knowing where to stop. Lola, after her swim, had put on her Sunday dress and was avoiding me, talking to Don Evaristo and his wife. The mayor, brandishing his staff, surrounded by Felipe and the police chief, was talking politics. My feeling of being out of place, which grew stronger at parties, sent me vagabonding several times to the spot Leticia had staked out. On one of those occasions, she gestured me forward.

"Go get us something to drink," she said. "Arístides and I are thirsty."

I went off to comply with the request. It was the first time I had heard Tuset's first name. Leticia had uttered it with such gravity that I thought I detected, deep down, a bit of bad faith. I found the name slightly ridiculous, like a suit that's too big. After examining the drinks table, I seized a bottle of white wine and took it to the fiancés. Leticia made me drink a glass with them and then sent me on my way with her silence.

Finally, in a corner of the patio, next to the deaf man and Tacuri, I got comfortable and started drinking steadily. The alliance formed by the three of us was not coincidental. You could say a secret affinity had brought us together. We were the only ones to watch the party with a kind of secret envy, of inner repulsion at joining in the general merriment. I didn't know why, but when we clinked glasses, I saw in their eyes a look of mute solidarity. A little later, my vision went blurry, the people became an errant troupe of actors, the party an absurd circulation of colors, and I the hub of a vast system of faces teeming around me.

Then I saw the unfolding of that great event, that long-awaited lunch where the eating was ferocious. The chicha had lit up faces and was soon forcing any vestige of politeness to beat a retreat. Renouncing forks, the guests grabbed pieces of chicken with their hands. In the end, the men took off their jackets, hawked up gobs of mucus, told dirty stories. At four in the afternoon, as the musicians sounded their cymbals, the guests were devouring with huge bites the last ears of corn. Inflamed by drink, Leonardo then challenged his guests to some target shooting. At the back of the patio a row of beer bottles was set up on high boxes and from the other end, lying on their bellies, the contestants raised their weapons. For half an hour shooting shook the cloisters, frightening the doves and causing the dogs to run off. The smell of gunpowder infested the air. The bullets sent splinters flying off the doors, pocked the walls; very few broke bottles. When the sun was going down and the sluggish body needed a brandy, we moved to the living room. It was, besides, time for the ceremony.

The evening cool had restored some of my lucidity. I managed to see then that the men, with that stiff seriousness usually adopted by the drunk, had gathered around the priest and Tuset's father. The latter was holding a small basket in whose interior gleamed two golden rings. Jisha served champagne in big, wide glasses. I heard comments indicating to me that the mayor was going to make a speech. The silence following the uproar seemed unreal to me.

At last, the mayor began to address the fiancés. It was one of those occasional speeches where it's normal to say serious things in a light tone. But the mayor had gotten the terms of the ritual backwards and was saying the most banal things in the tone of greatest solemnity. I hardly heard his words; instead, I observed Leticia's face. Her eyes fixed unblinking on the floor, she seemed to be listening stoically to a sermon. Her jaw was trembling slightly and it was impossible to tell if she was holding back a scream or a guffaw. Only when the mayor spoke of "future matrimony" did she dare raise her head and look around the room, resting her gaze insolently on Leonardo, who had found refuge in a distant corner of the room. When the mayor finished his speech to a storm of applause, Leticia remained withdrawn while Tuset, by her side, was shedding tears of emotion.

After putting on each other's rings, the fiancés received congratulations from the guests. It was an apotheosis of embraces. The band came in, and the party, interrupted for the ceremony, picked up again with furor. Leticia, making one last effort, tried to contribute to the collective euphoria, and several times I saw her smiling, dancing with her fiancé, her father, or the mayor. Every time a song ended there was a toast, whether to the harvest, to the mayor's office, to the engaged couple, or for whatever reason the inspiration of the moment could produce. In one of those silences, someone commented that the fiancés hadn't kissed, and a clamor broke out immediately in the living room, demanding that evidence of union. Leticia and Tuset were forced to fill their glasses and pushed into each other's arms. Tuset's lips advanced tremulously toward Leticia's, hesitated on the way, and at last rested on them in a long kiss. The shouts of joy and the tumult that greeted this happening prevented anyone from seeing that Leticia's hands were hanging rigidly at her side, so much so that from one of them fell her small bag of white beads and from the other her long scarlet shawl. Coarse shoes pulverized the sheer cloth and the beads. Everybody was staggering. Drunkenness was approaching its peak.

Taking advantage of the chaos, Leticia walked through the crowd and slipped out to one of the balconies. The atmosphere was charged with sweat, dust, clouds of smoke, and I was also tempted to cool off in the air from the road. When I got to the balcony, Leticia, who was leaning on the railing, turned around. Her face was greenish and a thread of spittle was hanging from her lips. I realized then she had vomited onto the road. I tried to offer her my handkerchief, but she rejected it and crossed the living room. As I got to the doorway, I saw her running toward her bedroom, leaving a trail of orange blossoms in the dark hallway.

NATURAL PHENOMENA

I was leaning on a column and watching the big heavy drops fall on the patio; I saw the earth getting wet, rivulets taking shape, torrents, waterfalls, true seas. A few hours of rain was all it took to reproduce in miniature, in rough terrain, the oldest geological processes. My admiring eyes followed the course of the water, saw how it greedily sought the slopes, how it pooled up behind a dam, dug a bed through a plain, made its way around an obstacle with a serpentine bend, joined another trickle to gain momentum, or divided into braids to go around an island. Soon the rain had formed on the patio a vast hydrographic system with mountains, basins, floods, infallible laws. Water collected in the stream running underneath the eaves of the tile roof, went out the gate, paralleled the road, rushed into a ditch, crossed the fields, nourished the crops, destroyed insects, strengthened the flow of a creek, and ended up dying in a swamp in the forest or with an energetic stroke that carried it to the ocean. Accustomed as I was to the fine mists of the coast, the spectacle of the rain fascinated me.

During those torrential days following Leticia's engagement, San Gabriel took on a tedious and mournful air. The bad weather forced us to wander through rooms that, after the guests' departure, seemed deprived of a fourth dimension. Everyone had left the day after the ceremony. Tuset and his family, the police chief, Aunt Mabila, and the deaf man left for Santiago. Don Evaristo, his wife, and Lola, for the interior.

Lola's departure was painful. Until the last minute she tried to get Leonardo to change his mind, but her pleas were futile. Just before mounting her horse, she broke the silence she had been stubbornly keeping toward me and embraced me effusively.

"If you ever have time, don't forget to pay me a visit," she whispered. "It will make my mother happy. It's only ten hours on horseback."

Felipe and I accompanied her for a stretch, walking beside her mount. When I saw her disappear around the first bend I felt truly sorry. I found out later that her mother was old and sick, that their coffee plants were louse-ridden, that in that ruinous, torrid, and gloomy setting she would probably have to spend the rest of her youth.

The very night of the ceremony, Leticia, for her part, had lain down proclaiming her decision to stay in bed for an indeterminate length of time. In vain did the travelers, especially her fiancé, insist on taking leave of her. Leticia refused to receive them, and for greater security she bolted the door to her bedroom. The only ones who had access to it were Alfredo and Julia.

In reality, apart from the fatigue of the engagement, she wasn't sick, but she exaggerated her condition, letting it be known that she was going to die, and had started to dictate, to Leonardo's great alarm, her last wishes. None of this prevented her from devouring with an appetite the food that Julia brought her or, in the evenings, when boredom got to be too much, from breaking out in song or dancing in her nightgown. What she wanted, at heart, was to recover the authority she lost by her engagement, to make her presence felt through isolation and extravagance.

Only once did she send Alfredo for me and was I able to go into her room. I found her lying on the bed, rolled up in a sheet, as if she already wanted to get used to the feeling of a shroud. Pointing me to a chair, she asked me with great solemnity to tell her a story. I came up with a story that she listened to absent-mindedly, her eyes on the ceiling, hands under the back of her head. Before I had finished she interrupted me to show me a notebook where colored stamps and drawings were pasted all together. She said it was her "collection," and there wasn't an envelope or magazine that went through her hands without suffering the tyranny of the scissors. But the strange thing is that I found her affectation natural, I didn't note the slightest trace of the ridiculous in her acts, and her behavior seemed to me perfectly coherent. She had her ring on the night table, along with the pieces of junk that amused her. When she picked it up, it was always to roll it over the bedspread.

When I asked her if she planned to give it back to him, she went quiet for a long time.

"How much could it have cost?" she asked me then. "If it was expensive I'd sell it and give the money to my father. I found out yesterday that he doesn't have any money and had to borrow from Don Evaristo.... Or if not, I'd give it to you so you could buy a horse. You're the only one who doesn't have a horse. In the summer you have to have one to go roaming around.... But why do I bother about these things? None of it matters to me! I've already said I'm going to die, in exactly one month I'm going to die."

As she said that, she covered her face with her hands and went still, not breathing.

"Like this, without realizing it, I'll die like this, with my eyes closed."

Since she remained silent, I started to leave.

"Wait!" she exclaimed. "Come here. I want to see something."

When I was next to her she examined me lengthily. Her gaze paused on every one of my features.

"Go on. Get out," she said, turning to the wall.

As I was walking out the door, she added:

"It looks like you got older after your trip to the river."

After five days the rains let up and several times I went with Leonardo to the potato fields. Tacuri, the foreman in charge of the laborers, came with us. The largest field was on a slightly sloping plain where a yellow sun shone and you inhaled a rarefied mountain air. It was the highest part of the hacienda, but it was also the only part whose lay-out and size permitted extensive cultivation. A row of gray rocks sheltered it from the chill winds blowing down from the mines.

We tied the horses to a stake and went into the field. Leonardo paused constantly to examine a plant, pull it up, feel the tuber. Tacuri said that within two weeks, at the latest, the harvest should start. The two of them started arguing about things I didn't understand. My great diversion was to look around me from the middle of the field and to feel myself rocked by that limitless panorama of greenery. Because of the wind the plants undulated in a way that recalled the swell of the ocean. Then we would keep going. Birds took flight when they sensed our approach, and Tacuri ran after them, throwing dirt clods or imitating the barking of a dog.

One morning the valley was unusually calm. It wasn't just the sun piercing the hazy glare or the sky fixing its limpid blue pupil on us. It was a kind of motionlessness, of petrifaction, that nature seemed to have undergone. No breezes blew, the trees weren't breathing, objects cast clear and unfeeling shadows.

Felipe, who was in the study dictating a letter to me, interrupted himself several times to look off the balcony. Once he went to the railing and stood looking for a long time at the eucalyptus grove.

"How strange!" he murmured. "It's as if the earth had stopped turning."

That was, in fact, the feeling you got from the landscape: stopped, rigid, something like cardboard scenery. Leonardo, who was wandering through the arcades, had the same impression. The three of us remained on the patio gazing at the sky, through which one disorderly flock of doves after another migrated east.

The calm continued until near noon. Jacinto must have been nervous because his fists resounded several times on the door. Leonardo, used to those protests by then, ignored him. He had worked out the plan to put him in an asylum and to move him there he was only waiting for some money.

Just before lunch, the dogs, which had been dozing until then, woke up restless. Zarco ran around the patio sniffing the air, clawing the earth. For a while he growled and jumped around us, pursuing us with his phosphorescent eyes. The Negro Reynaldo said that the dogs were seeing the devil and that if we spread the sleep from their eyes on ours we would die of fright.

When lunch started we were all suffering from a feeling of unease, and bent over the table, heedful of the slightest noise from the fields, we gulped our spoonfuls of soup in silence. Felipe, exasperated by this situation, was the first to speak up, and he started telling a story. His voice was beginning to distract us when Leonardo, with an energetic gesture, asked him to be quiet. We all pricked our ears and we heard then the birth of a low, distant rumble, like that of an underground river. The noise was getting louder. The water in the decanter started moving back and forth. As I looked at the wall clock I saw that the pendulum was hitting hard on both sides of the box. When the first chunk of plaster fell off the ceiling we all stood up and ran for the patio. The ground had started to shake.

The shaking probably didn't last for more than a minute, but that lapse of time seemed to me devoid of all measure, without beginning or end, and capable of containing, like the time of a nightmare, a multitude of successive fates.

The first tremors were so strong that the ground seemed to undulate, and as we were running down the hall I stumbled and Aunt Ema fell. Someone must have helped her up, because later we all met in the middle of the patio, bunched together one moment, scattered out of control the next, constantly shouting, tottering, shaking our arms like marionettes. The subterranean rumbling was growing and growing, so much so that our voices could barely be heard amid the howling of the dogs. Leticia had emerged wrapped in a blanket; she was hanging on Leonardo's arm and crying. Ema, on her knees, was hitting her breast and praying out loud. Leonardo, silent, watched tiles come loose and break into pieces on the ground. Some cracks opened in the ground and in the walls. The window panes shattered. The shouting of the Indians was hair-raising. The carpenter Tobías was looking for his children in the tumult. Leonardo remembered Jacinto and, after running to his room, came back pulling him by the arm. The outline of the hills seemed to fade away, and thick dust clouds rose along the slopes. Felipe had lit a cigarette and was asking for calm, shouting that it was a natural phenomenon, but nobody was listening to him and his own voice seemed to betray him. The first wall to collapse, with an awful creaking sound, was one in the carpentry workshop. "Who's missing? Who's missing?" a voice repeated. Someone remembered Marica. The rumble disappeared at times to start up again suddenly and redouble our terror. "Someone's got to go get Marica," screeched Ema. The dust storm was moving off the hills, spreading through the air, and blowing toward the house in big dust devils. The stable door collapsed and the horses, neighing, showed up on the patio. When Ema shouted for Marica the third time, Felipe threw his cigarette to the ground and started for the hall. The ground was still shaking intermittently when he went inside under a shower of plaster. "You're crazy!" someone shouted. The last shock tilted the chapel belfry. We all saw how slowly it started leaning more and more to one side, without losing its form, until it fell to the ground and became dust. Jacinto had broken out laughing.

His guffaws were the last sounds we heard. We had all gone quiet feeling the last tremors fade away underfoot. Silent, pale, we looked at each other, recognized each other, congratulated each other with gestures; we could have hugged each other or broken out crying. The morning calm was reborn, but the setting had changed. The sun went on shining through fine floating dust that made us cough and what it illuminated was only a parody of what had been.

We exploded into comment simultaneously. We were all talking at the same time, the notion of hierarchy lost. But what we were saying didn't make sense, because the quake seemed to have shaken our consciences, agitated our inner worlds, and we emerged struggling in the midst of ruined words. Someone managed to mention Felipe's name and we went quiet again, looking at the hall. Nobody dared take a step. Ema, followed by Leonardo, was the first to make a move. Before they made it to the cloister Felipe reappeared, crunching fragments of roof tile under his boots. His head and shoulders were dusted with plaster, and in his right arm, as if he were dealing with a rag doll, he was carrying Marica.

"She's alive and kicking," he murmured nervously.

But a shout coming from the other end caught our attention. Tobías and his wife were nosing about the ruins and scratching at the ground. It seemed that something was lying buried and fleeing them. When a small white arm with its fingers pointing toward the sky emerged, I turned around and ran to the gate. Then I found myself wandering breathlessly over the fresh wounds of the country.

THE MOLLEPATA ROAD

*A*long with some newspapers that Mabila sent, the first batch of mail that came from Santiago did much to restore our peace of mind. The quake had involved only the northern highlands and only a slight tremor had been felt in Lima. The death toll still hadn't been calculated, but it was assumed that it would not exceed one thousand.

There was talk of donations, aid from the Red Cross, army planes that dropped food and medicine, volunteers who were coming forward to help the victims. When they dealt with these matters, the papers used moving language. I was touched as I read them, and in the midst of so many pronouncements and sermons on solidarity, I had the illusion that our country was not an aggregate of people who didn't know and mistrusted each other but a perfect fatherland stricken in the heart. But our mourning would last as long as a feeling lasts. A few months later, probably, we would be dancing on the bellies of our dead.

Ten days later, when Leonardo started energetically supervising the rebuilding, the catastrophe had lost all prestige with us. The papers kept talking about it, but the headlines were getting smaller and smaller. Our anguishing experience was being stripped of the terror it had held for us and turning at last into the smallest trifle an experience can boil down to: a date. When the first joke came—it was said that the Japanese had sent us the earthquake in reprisal for the recent assaults on their grocery stores—we laughed happily. We were laughing openly at fate. It was time to go on to something else.

But calamities never arrive alone. Once the breach is made, they call each other and soon are legion. Several dry, cloudless days of burning sunshine followed the quake. At night, the clear sky revealed all its constellations and we spent hours face-up, receiving a distant light that turned us pale. Leonardo couldn't make up his mind about the harvest, hoping that the tubers would get heavier. Bonfires of sawdust and kerosene were lit at night to protect the plants. In the living room, the image of Saint Gabriel, the local patron saint of the harvest, was invoked, and Leonardo, with a very particular faith, approached the saint between two glasses of pisco to hit himself absent-mindedly in the chest.

It was all in vain. When a few leaves in the high part of the field started going black and the cuticle on the stem split, Leonardo rushed to bring in the harvesters from Angasmarca. About a hundred field hands arrived and put up their shelters around the hacienda. The potato harvest began.

Leonardo and Felipe would leave at dawn, eat in the fields, and not come back until evening. They were both unshaven and had rings around their eyes. When they sat down for dinner they seemed to be in the mood for arguing. Tacuri, as the foreman, was an obligatory dinner guest at this period, and he ate with us without removing his poncho and drank of the master's chicha. The predominating opinion was that, given the smallness of the potatoes, much of the harvest would have to be sold for seed. Felipe often dropped out of the discussions and remained plunged in thought, as if under the sway of a fixed idea.

When I went up to the plateau, I saw the fields transformed by the hands of the laborers. The potatoes had emerged from the earth and formed huge hillocks that were worked over by the Indian women. The plowmen arrived with their beasts of burden. There were mules, llamas, donkeys. The potatoes were transported to the hacienda. In the patio they were separated according to size, to quality, and after getting put into sacks and weighed they were taken to the storehouse.

The traders from Santiago and Mollepata supervised the weighing, argued with Leonardo. Then they went to the study, where they drank until evening as they went over the numbers. Vicuña, a fat and rich half-breed, owner of forty mules, got for his cash most of the harvest. Leonardo cursed his bad luck and said that with a road and a truck he would not only eliminate the middlemen but also put his products more cheaply in the hands of the consumer.

On Saturday evenings the harvesters came down and filled the patio. Since they didn't know how to sign their names, they would leave their fingerprints in the payroll. Most of them spent the night at the hacienda, spread out over the grounds. At nightfall they formed circles where they joked, drank, and sang lively *huaynos*.

Leticia watched them with scorn. For several days, forgetting her oaths, she had been up and was wandering from one place to another engaged in completely pointless activity. She meddled in everything, wanting to give orders, as if intending to replace Aunt Ema or do her work. She was authoritarian with the harvesters, wild, finding a kind of voluptuousness in despotism. She knew a few insults in Quechua and used them with prodigality. Sometimes she had fun throwing a handful of cigarettes and watching the Indians and roll over the ground and fight for them.

"Those lousy animals are going to infect the whole house!" she was constantly shouting.

This behavior soon bored her. Since nobody took her theatrics seriously, she changed her methods. She became generous. Rummaging through her old clothes, she took great pains to dress up a small Indian girl as a young lady. One night I discovered her handing out, behind Leonardo's back, a few bottles of brandy that the old women thanked her for by kissing her hand.

Toward the end of the harvest, we received an unexpected visit; the gringa María showed up one morning at the hacienda. She was skinny, burned by the mountain sun, with locks of straw-colored hair falling over her forehead. She had walked from the Huaylas gorge, putting up at night in the roadside inns. She said that Daniel had died in the earthquake, and whimpering she asked us to put her up. Nobody believed her; the rumor was rather that her husband must have fled her as if from a cataclysm.

Her presence created a climate of discord. From the start Ema was against taking her in, alleging that Daniel might come back and the fights would start up again. Felipe seemed discomfited by the situation, and with no gratitude toward his former lover, he maintained an incriminating silence. Leonardo, on the other hand, decided to give her a room and treated her with a politeness that left us all astonished. From then on she was at the table again, complaining about everything in her out-of-tune voice, gazing plaintively with her colorless eyes into Felipe's impassive face. She would spend almost the whole day sitting in the doorway to her room, knitting something or other, sneaking one look after another at the movement around the hacienda. Nights, she drank too much and you could hear her wandering through the arcades until late. When she went by our room, Felipe smiled:

"If you want to sleep with a woman, all you have to do is talk to that old hen."

In one of the many after-dinner conversations, the gringa asked unexpectedly after Tuset. At the sound of that name there was an embarrassed silence. I realized then that for a long time nobody had talked about him at all. He had been banished from our talks, and that measure—whose origin was mysterious—revealed, more than indifference, the progress of some conspiracy. When Leticia and her brothers left, Leonardo, who had answered the gringa in vague terms, exploded:

"I don't even want to see that idiot! He didn't give any signs of life after the earthquake. For a few days I thought he'd died and I killed myself trying to find out what happened. And you know what? He went to Huamachuco without even asking about us."

"He could have sent a letter or a telegram," added Ema. "That's how you can tell he's the son of a storekeeper."

"There's something else," continued Leonardo. "And this is just between us. Tuset has a mistress."

His declaration left us unmoved. Felipe, who couldn't stand serious situations, put in one of his epigrams.

"It would be strange if he didn't have one. At his age, a man without a mistress has something wrong with him."

"It's not a laughing matter," replied Leonardo dryly. "It's serious because he has three children by her. Besides, the woman is bad, a drunken stallkeeper who does what she wants with him and even slaps him around, so I've heard."

Ema started shrieking. She said that they had to send the mayor a letter breaking off the engagement, that they had to let Leticia know. In her fit of indignation she even wanted to burn the mattress Tuset had slept on.

"Lord knows what diseases he has!" she said, scratching her arms as if she were already infected.

"Better not to say anything to Leticia," put in Leonardo. "That way we can avoid hard explanations. I have to go to Santiago with the kids and while I'm there I'll give the mayor a piece of my mind. And let's not talk about this anymore."

As a result of that revelation I remained confused for several days. In fact, what I experienced was the birth of an irresistible pleasure that I was afraid to admit to myself. In one way or another, as part of a whim or through her disdain, Tuset had always had a privileged place in Leticia's inner world. I had simply orbited him, like a beggar picking up a kiss now and then, a stray scratch. Now things had changed. With Tuset out of the way, the road was clear.

But I couldn't make up my mind to set down it. All I managed was to adopt a policy of servility toward Leticia. I walked in her shadow heedful of her slightest whims. I went down into the ravines and came back with the reddest prickly pears to give to her. Other times I carved in saponite animal heads that she accepted with cries of fright. My gifts were always given in silence and I refused even her gratitude. At times it seemed to me all I wanted was to make myself indispensable, make her need me, and so enter the routine of her joys.

This tactic had results, because Leticia started honoring me with somewhat more trust. Sometimes she would talk to me for a long time, naturally, as if she could relax in my company. One morning she decided to go down the Mollepata road with me.

I had gotten in the habit of going on a morning walk with Jacinto. He had been better for several weeks. His anger appeased, his fits of destruction forgotten, Jacinto was allowed by Leonardo to wander around the patio, and at last he agreed to let me take him around the hacienda. The Mollepata road was my favorite because it was full of Spanish broom, blackberries, and because there were deep gorges falling toward hot valleys where the vegetation grew dense and wild.

When we set off Leticia was happy. Taking Jacinto by both arms, we pulled him along any way we wanted, making him jump over ditches. The two of us were singing and Jacinto, caught up by our enthusiasm, let out howls that disturbed the bulls in their pastures. When the sun started heating up, we lay down on the grass to rest. Face up, gazing at the sky, we followed with our fingers the changing shapes of the passing clouds. Suddenly I noticed that Leticia had gone quiet. When I turned toward her, I saw her leaning up on her elbow, her brow wrinkled, looking intently at me. She must have been looking like that for a long time. Her expression made me shudder.

"The game is up," she said seriously. "Now you're going to tell me what's going on."

As I didn't manage a reply, she leaned over Jacinto and grabbed me by the wrist.

"Don't play the fool! Tell me what's happening with Tuset."

I stammered for a second. All I was thinking then was that all Leticia's trust had been a farce to destined to elicit confidences from me. Once again I felt myself beaten at my own game.

"I don't know what you're talking about," I replied.

Her hand let freed my wrist.

"You want to lie to me too," she whispered, and I noticed such a tone of disappointment in her voice that I was moved. My doubts lasted a few seconds. I realized then that keeping quiet about Tuset's behavior was idiotic and that telling Leticia about it would create between us a small exchange of secrets that I might one day profit from.

"Tuset has a woman," I answered brutally.

Leticia looked at me confused, as if she didn't understand.

"She's a stallkeeper from Huamachuco that he's got three children with."

Leticia's eyes seemed to flee and remained floating in space. Her fingers had traveled up to her lips. I watched her with repressed anxiety, almost regretting what I had said. At last she turned toward me and examined me attentively. It was as if she were trying to study me, to uncover some hidden idea. I felt ashamed just then and I told myself that if she could read my thoughts she might hate me for the rest of her life.

"You can be happy now," she murmured.

I tried to open my mouth, but she stopped me.

"Don't talk!" she said, lying back down on the grass.

I didn't want to interrupt her so I turned toward Jacinto. He had fallen asleep with his arm over his eyes. I stared at his beard, the small veins in his face, making an effort to find something interesting in that mask.

"You should go," said Leticia. "You should go to the bottom of that gorge and bring me a bouquet of broom."

As I didn't make a move, she insisted.

"Didn't you hear? Go on and get me a bunch of broom. The vases in the chapel are empty. We have to arrange them this evening."

I ran down the slope. I spent a long time throwing rocks into the river and watching the pools go muddy. I was restless, humiliated by having obeyed, without resisting, those capricious orders. Then I ventured into the thicket and sought out the darkest places, like an injured animal. When I was out of breath I picked the yellow flowers and went back up the gorge.

Jacinto was still asleep, but Leticia's place was empty. After taking a look around I saw her sitting next to an agave that extended its thorny arms over her. Her eyes were fixed on the ground. When she saw me approach she didn't say a word. Nor when she took the flowers I held out to her.

"Help me get up," she muttered at last, holding out her arms.

Taking her by the hand, I pulled hard. When she was in front of me she looked into my eyes. She looked as though she had just abandoned a dream.

"Have to go on a trip," she mumbled.

I tried to pull her to me, but she pulled away energetically.

"Let's go," she said, walking toward Jacinto.

We went back without a word. Jacinto was the only one talking, complaining about the sun because he hadn't brought his hat. At times I was glad he was with us, because his presence isolated us from each other and justified our silence. Before we got home, Leticia stopped, smelled the bouquet of broom, and threw it over a wall.

"Tomorrow at seven I'll be waiting for you in the loft," she said, taking the lead and going through the gate alone.

Sun-Struck Prickly Pear

*T*he next morning, when I was getting ready to go to the cows for my first drink from the milking, Felipe, who was already up, kept me in his side of the room. A bottle on his night table told me he had decided to breakfast on pisco that morning. As he poured the alcohol into a cup, he told me he had had an argument with Leonardo the night before and had made up his mind to leave the hacienda.

"What I want to know is this," he added. "You came with me to the hacienda so I'm responsible for you. What do you plan to do?"

His question unsettled me. I didn't feel just then like examining my situation in detail and I told him I was planning to stay.

"What for? What are you going to do here? It would be better if you came with me. You know how I live, going around here and there. But you'll have a change of scenery and you won't get bored. I'm telling you from experience that it's no good staying in one place for a long time. I'm going to Chanchamayo now to set up a sawmill."

"I want to help Leonardo," I answered resolutely. "It wouldn't be good to leave him just now."

"Very nice, that gesture of yours, but off the wall! How can you help Leonardo? What he needs is money. He's in debt up to his neck. He's going to go to Santiago today to see if he can get a loan from the bank. If he doesn't get it he'll have to mortgage the hacienda. In the end, this is all falling apart. I'm like a rat that can smell the sinking ship."

"It doesn't matter," I answered stubbornly. "I'm staying."

"Do whatever you want," he exclaimed peevishly, leaning back on his pillow. His gaze traveled over the roof-beams. His half-closed eyes, his ruddy cheeks, signaled to me that the alcohol was working its effects. As a rule, Felipe never got drunk, but by his third drink he went into a kind of contemplative mood interrupted by brief fits of violence that restored the equilibrium.

Taking advantage of his silence, I was starting to leave when I heard him call me.

"Is there not any other reason you want to stay?"

I thought about asking him to explain what he meant, but he waved me away with a vague movement of his hand.

"At your age I was worse," he said. "But stop playing games and get to the point. The gazelle is loose and around here there are plenty of stealthy hunters."

When I went out to the patio Leonardo was already in his riding clothes, ready to leave for Santiago. Ollanta and Alfredo were also going. At the last minute he had decided to take them with him. Ollanta would stay at school in Santiago and Alfredo would be sent to the Chiclayo military academy.

The farewell was of a coldness that left me dismayed. I had expected a touching scene, but Alfredo was dry and the only person he hugged effusively was Leticia. He settled for shaking my hand, mumbling something about how he hoped to see me when he came back.

From then on I wandered around the patio in search of something to do. After the recent incidents, the meeting arranged by Leticia took on importance again and became my only justification for that day. I was in the smithy watching the Negro Reynaldo hammer a pair of tongs into shape, but I soon realized that the wait would only be tolerable if I attacked time at its roots, that is, in my own nature.

The immediate surroundings of the hacienda were all familiar to me, but there was one place I hadn't gone back to since the beginning of my stay: the hill with the cross. I had heard people say that you could find viscachas around the summit, and grabbing a shotgun and a game bag from the gunroom, I set off.

After fording the river, I started up the hill by the steepest shortcuts. Several times I was on the point of falling off cliffs. Just before reaching the shelter I saw the Indian girl Julia picking bunches of wild spearmint. I stood next to her for a long time, watching how she bent over to reveal the dark nape of her neck, inviting you to lay hands on it. Little by little she walked away, turning around now and then. In the end she was just a dot retained by my pupils. I woke up then, as if from a spell of lethargy, surprised to feel the cold of the shotgun on my palm.

When I got to the summit I started exploring the rocks in search of viscachas. My efforts were futile: never in my life had I seen a viscacha. Disappointed, exhausted, prey to an inexplicable sadness, I sat down next to the cross. It must have been noon. The sun was beating down on my head.

From that spot I could see all of the San Gabriel valley; you might say I could capture it in the palm of my hand. The roads intersected in front of the hacienda, forming a huge, wild cross. You could see the road to Santiago as it crossed ravines and pastures and petered out in a long red esplanade at the gate of the house; you could also see the Mollepata road, rich in prickly pear, in lemon trees, in big bright flowers that signaled proximity to hot lowland valleys; the path to the mine wound around the cemetery and rose abruptly, through rock and abyss, to the chill heights; the Huayrurán gorge, last, was like a crevice in the thorny bad-lands sloping down toward the southern hills.

I had traveled all those roads several times: on foot, on Peruvian burros, to the trot of long-suffering mules. There wasn't a single bend that hadn't been the object of my curiosity. All my afternoons of laziness or rancor were scattered out there. I remembered rocks, lots of rocks, seeds fallen at the foot of the trees, clumps of blackberry bushes, moss from the ditches, wet and fallen tree trunks, and the prickly pear barrens, the endless the prickly pear barrens. It was all beautiful and too big for mere words. When I thought that beyond the horizon were more mountains, more trees, more animals, more houses, more rocks, and so on, more and more, indefinitely, I told myself that one language wasn't enough, that you would need all the languages on earth to sing such greatness.

I was standing up, leaning on the cross. My hands caressed the rough-hewn wood, old wood that had lost its resin. When I took a close look at it I saw the initials and dates carved in its skin by all the residents of the valley. My enthusiasm fled through a strange fissure. In an instant, that grandiose land that I had dreamed of started to fill with human faces and not all of them were good, desirable, or happy. Corruption also sprang from the land. I imagined that there must be other valleys like San Gabriel, with their masters and servants, their uprisings, their orgies, their hunting grounds, their madmen locked in towers. My sadness dominated me again, and unable to take hold of myself I stood inert for a long time, discouraged, pressing with my gaze the pointless beauty, the desperate greenery of the land.

It was only when I heard the mill that I realized I was close to the house. When I paused I vaguely remembered having descended the hill with great strides, having eaten ripe prickly pears at the foot of a tall hawthorn, having had fulminating visions like someone hallucinating. In front of the gate I couldn't make up my mind about going in. I was ashamed to go back to the house with an empty bag. Looking around me, I saw a goldfinch on a rock wall and without hesitating I brought it down with a single shot. When I went to pick it up I saw a thin trickle of blood coming from its open beak. I didn't want to touch it and I left it lying there on the grass.

By evening I was in the smithy again. The heat from the furnace was suffocating. Reynaldo, covered with sweat and sparks, seemed to me, at times, a hellish vision, reminding me of the image of Vulcan I had seen years before in a book of engravings. I felt feverish, besides, as if the sun had put some curse on my blood.

Toward dusk I found myself in the loft, walking around and around a bunch of old junk. I had been led there more by a dark instinct than by a deliberate act of will. I knew that Leticia would come, but I wasn't thinking about her or about anything. My head was throbbing and large drops of sweat burned my forehead. I soon dropped into the hay, feeling an invincible pressure on my eyelids.

When it was almost completely dark, Leticia showed up. Her silhouette crossed the threshold and glided toward me. She sat down on the straw and remained silent. Shadows came in through the attic windows and lay down at our feet.

"You didn't come to lunch today," she said at last.

I tried to tell her that I had been on the hill, but I realized it would take a huge effort to tell her what it was I had gone up there looking for and what I had found. I put out my hand and took hers, which I held to my chest.

"You're burning up!" she added. And leaning over, she blew on my forehead as if she wanted to put out a hot coal. You must have pushed yourself too much."

Her breath went into my nose. I suddenly leaned up on my elbow.

"I've been waiting for this moment the whole day," I told her. "I was in the smithy, up on the hill, and the hours seemed so long to me."

"Ssh!" she answered, making a gesture with her hand. "Don't talk."

There was another pause. I felt nothing but Leticia's cold hand on my burning one and the rhythm of our breathing.

"What's wrong with you?" she asked me. "You seem to have a fever. You're shaking from head to toes. Did you get chilled?"

"You're right, I have a fever…. It was the sun, the prickly pears."

"You should go and lie down. We'll bring some spearmint to your bed. We'll talk tomorrow."

"No!" I protested. "I don't want to go downstairs. I want to stay up here. I'm going to sleep here on the straw. I'm going to spend the night here."

"It freezes at dawn."

The cold was starting to travel up from my feet.

"It freezes at dawn and you can die."

I had dropped back into the straw. Blood throbbed in my temples. Something like luminous fish swam in front of my eyes.

"At least tell me what you came up for."

Leticia got up. In the darkness I could barely make out her shadow circling me.

"I told you yesterday," she whispered. "I'm thinking about taking a trip. I'm tired of San Gabriel. I have nothing to do here."

"Felipe's going too!" I interrupted her. "Everybody's leaving. I might leave too."

"That's just it. I was thinking about going to my cousins' house in Lima. Leonardo won't let me go alone. But it'll be different if he knows you're with me."

"Is that really what he says?"

"Yes."

For a moment I was baffled. Mentally, in a fraction of a second, I imagined the whole trip, I saw the mountain range, the truck rolling through the mud, the dunes, and I felt the weariness of the road.

"We'll see the ocean from the window," I said. "You know on the coast there are small towns where they sell fruit and sweets to people traveling. The road is like a ribbon of tar unrolling itself through the dunes."

"We'll travel together," replied Leticia. "But in Lima we won't see each other. I'll live with my girl cousins."

Her last words hurt me. Leticia had sat back down by my side.

"Why do you say that?"

"They're rich. They have a big house and yard. I'll spend all my time with them."

"You're just like everybody else," I exclaimed, turning toward the wall. I would have liked to have been alone just then. I was distressed. It must have been the fever. My teeth were chattering.

Leticia took me by the shoulders.

"You don't know me," she said, speaking with unusual haste. "I once took a trip to the mine, six hours around the cliffs—remember? I do things like that, without thinking. I'll say one thing and do something different. I like to change my mind, or I change it from one minute to the next…. Don't you realize that I?…"

Abruptly, she interrupted herself. Her hands had slid along my shoulders and seemed to be seeking my throat. Just then I felt an irrepressible fear.

"Let go!" I shouted, trying to push her away.

She kept feeling my throat.

"Why are you scared? You have a vein here that's throbbing. And you're all sweaty! You should go downstairs. Obey me and tomorrow I'll be nice to you."

Her hands left me. Everything was mixed up in my conscience. Without putting up resistance, I let her lead me by the arm. I soon found myself standing up. We had barely taken a few steps when I felt Leticia pushing me against the wall and pressing up against me with her body. A noise was coming from the ladder.

"Someone's coming up," she whispered.

A light started dancing in the room next door. We heard the sound of muffled footsteps and sibilant breathing. Leticia leaned back and looked through the doorway.

"It's Jisha!"

"Is he stealing?"

Her hand covered my mouth. I felt her lips brush my ear.

"He's coming to get corn for the hens."

I remembered that in the next room there was a mound of corn. The sound of the grains falling to the bottom of the sack reached us. The work seemed endless.

Leticia had rested her cheek on mine. Her bust was shaking. One night, before I left for the mine, I had had her like that, at my mercy, in my room. But I was strong then. Now I could barely lift my arms to hold her. The sound of the corn stopped. The light went out. The footsteps sounded farther and farther away.

"It's time to go down," said Leticia, pulling away. "I'll go first and then whistle to you from downstairs."

I sat down in the loft waiting for her signal. I felt aerial and weightless, as if my insides had been emptied. I don't remember if Leticia whistled or not. The fact is, I suddenly found myself in the hall, gliding toward my room. When I made it to the arcades, I stumbled and fell senseless to the paving stones.

THE WALTZ

I convalesced in a lawn chair in the quietest corner of the patio. The hours were soft there, and the life of the hacienda, crossing the great sunny space, reached me in slow, silent waves. At times I saw Leonardo emerge from the study and glide through the arcades. Other times it was Felipe who arose from the shadows to yawn at the sky or light a cigarette or the gringa María crossing the patio diagonally with quick steps, looking behind her again and again. But the only presence capable of breaking the calm and disturbing me was Leticia's. Catching sight of her in the hall was all it took for things to immediately take on a positional value: a rock she might stumble on, a column that momentarily took her from my sight. When she was next to me, she would gesture, and I would get out of my chair to follow her.

We would meet behind the kitchen and the chicken coops in a kind of empty lot shaded by a polylepis tree. Julia was always present at our meetings, to which, by one of Leticia's designs, we gave a certain air of mystery. We looked over the map of the province, our cheeks very close together, our thumbs wandering along the roads. Leticia asked me seriously about hotels, buses, the cost of living in the coastal cities. When I talked to her about Lima she listened to me attentively, interrupting me to have me repeat some detail that she would take meticulous note of in her mind. I enjoyed these interviews as long as Julia was around, but Leticia soon managed to make her disappear. That's when things got awkward. I tried in vain to start talking again about our plans. The map, unfolded before our eyes, stopped being a road map and turned into a pretext for our closeness. Little by little, we sensed its presence bothering us, accusing us, and we would let it slide to our feet. Then Julia would reappear and we would start playing the travelers again.

On one occasion Leticia showed up with a basket wrapped in a napkin. Unwrapping it, she uncovered a dish of potatoes, hot peppers, and a bottle of chicha. After we drank it we felt drowsy, and jumping over a rock wall we headed into the pasture. Lying down next to each other, we slept while Julia watched over our rest. From that day on, Leticia always showed up at our meetings with a bottle of chicha. Sometimes she would bring a cigarette that she smoked clumsily. The nap in the country became a ritual. When we woke up we discovered our bodies very close together, as if they had sought each other during our sleep.

Those days of rest, of weakness, of small pastoral exaltations, caused me to have less to do with the other residents of San Gabriel.

Because of my illness, they all seemed to me to take on a kind of ghost-like existence. But recovering my strength was all it took for my curiosity to reawaken, and I peered out of myself, avid for life and all the transformations of life.

Felipe held my attention. He had lost his poise and become a grumpy and impatient man. At the table he didn't talk to anybody, and the evenings he spent in his side of the room kicking the furniture. When he emerged, it was always in the direction of one of the roadside taverns, from which he returned late with a discreet drunkenness that would let him sleep soundly.

"I don't even have money for cigarettes!" I often heard him complain. "Can you believe it? And I was tipping the waiters in Trujillo fifty *soles*!"

When I asked him what he was waiting for to leave San Gabriel, he would go into a rage.

"You think I'm staying here because I want to? If it were up to me I'd have been gone a long time ago! The problem is Leonardo hasn't paid me. I've been waiting for three weeks. I don't know how long it'll take. He's going to mortgage the hacienda and the engineers haven't even come for the appraisal."

They came from Santiago one sunny morning. Their presence caused a minor stir and San Gabriel seemed to recover its former majesty. There were feasts, outings, tests of agility. Leonardo blew everything he had left on a party. His tactic was to impress the experts with the appearance of a bonanza. Brandy flowed in torrents. The engineers spent most of their time drunk. One of them split open his head against a table. The other one drank until he collapsed and on a night of wine tried to rape one of the cooks. The eve of their departure there was a big party that lasted until dawn. Early in the morning, Leonardo helped them mount their horses, stuffed their saddlebags with hams, and sent them off to Santiago like two postal messengers.

"I hope they have good memories of their visit," he said, watching them trot crazily away, trailing a cloud of dust.

One evening Felipe burst out:

"I can't take it anymore!" he said, approaching me. "I've got to get out of here! It's taking so long I'm going to lose my job at the sawmill. Go see Leonardo right now and ask him how long I'm going to have to wait. I don't want to talk to him because we'll end up arguing. Go on.... And if you can get me a cigarette."

I left the bedroom and headed for the study. Leonardo was neither there nor in the living room or the dining room. I went back to the cloister and started looking through all the buildings around the house. In the gun room I ran into the Negro Reynaldo.

"He went to the stables," he told me.

It had gotten dark. Before going through the gate I heard the horses whinnying. For a long time I wandered around the mangers breathing in that thick smell of fresh straw and manure. I was getting ready to leave when I heard voices coming from a water tank. There was an old well somewhere around there. Without hesitating, I headed over, but after a few steps I stopped short. Leonardo, sitting on the curbstone, had his arms around a woman.

I turned around and fled toward the patio. I just about knocked down Jacinto, who was observing the sky with a telescope.

"Look," he said, taking me by the arm. "Over the hills there, toward the left, you can see a red blinking star."

When I took the telescope my hands were shaking.

"What's wrong?" he asked me.

Not even I could have answered him. I was still thinking about the silhouette I had seen stuck to Leonardo's body. I thought I had recognized a local girl's shawl.

"I can't see anything." I answered him.

"There! Look there! Over the hills! Can't you see it? It's a red star with a long tail. It's a comet; it's like a sign that something's going to happen one of these days. Something that will change everything!"

I couldn't spot anything because, in reality, I had other things in mind.

"You should clean the lens," I answered him, retreating to the living room.

I dropped into an armchair and sat there stunned. I thought Leonardo would have to pass by there. Mechanically, I approached the record player and put on a record. The music started to distract me. It was the old waltz Leticia had danced to the first Sunday I spent in San Gabriel.

> The night that in the dance
> your eyes locked on mine....

I remembered her twirling in Tuset's arms. A strange convulsion gripped my heart. It was nothing in particular, just the feeling of elapsed time, of the irretrievable past. More images, attracted as if by magnetization, congregated around the first one.

Who can it be? Who can it be?
I ask myself ceaselessly....

I saw Lola's big eyes as she murmured those trivial verses over and over. The perfume of her clothes hurt my nose. I needed to see her, to talk to her, and I was already starting an imaginary dialogue when I heard footsteps in the living room. When I looked up I saw Aunt Ema, who had stopped a few steps from the doorway.

"Did you put on that record," she asked, approaching me.

"Yes."

"Why did you put it on?"

"I don't know."

Ema stopped by my side. She didn't take her eyes off me. In their depths I could make out a sad examination, a difficult irony. My anxiety grew. I wished someone would come in and interrupt us.

"Let's dance," she said, holding an arm out to me.

At first I thought she was joking, but when she took me by the hand I couldn't refuse. She pulled me to her and objects started going around. The big empty space let us move quickly. One after another I saw the record player, the balcony, the dining room, the patio....

"Are you scared?" she said to me all at once. "Why? Are you always scared of women?"

The record player, the balcony, the dining room, the patio....

"I want to know something," she went on. I'm more than thirty years old and I could be your mother...."

The record player, the balcony, the dining room, the patio....

"You won't lie to me because you're still a boy...."

The record player, the balcony, the dining room, the patio....

"What do you two go behind the chicken coop for? You're there every afternoon."

The record player, the balcony, the dining room, the patio....

"You meet Leticia there. What do you talk about?"

The record player, the balcony, the dining room, the patio....

"You must talk about yourselves, the things you talk about when you're sixteen."

The record player, the balcony, the dining room, the patio....

"About great love, that's it, about the great loves of youth!"

The music stopped. We still managed to spin around once more. The needle was scratching the dead part of the record. We soon stopped. I wasn't able to answer anything.

"Listen," continued Ema. "I don't want anything to happen between you and Leticia. I don't have any authority over her to give her advice. But you're a reasonable person and you might pay attention to me. It wouldn't bother me at all if you and Leticia weren't first cousins. Things between relatives never turn out right. Look at Jacinto, Aníbal, who threw himself into the river. Their parents were related. They married each other to combine two farms and make an hacienda. I've always lived with abnormal people. Leticia herself…."

Jacinto entered just then. Ema, who had taken my arm, let go of me.

"Lucho!" exclaimed Jacinto. "Are you coming? The sky's clearer now, you can see better now."

Ema left the room quickly. I looked at Jacinto without replying.

"Why don't you want to come? You're mad at me, you don't like me anymore. Leonardo doesn't either. I just saw him coming back from the water tank with Julia. He says I'm an idiot."

"Where's Leonardo?"

"He went into the study."

"Wait," I said, and left the room.

Leonardo was standing next to his desk. When he saw me come in he looked at me rather inquisitively for a moment.

"Were you in the manger?" he asked.

"No," I replied firmly.

"Someone was walking around there," he added, turning on his heels to gaze out the window. I remained in suspense, not knowing what to say to him. I thought about the bodies embraced on the curbstone of the well.

"I need a cigarette," was all I managed to say.

"You're smoking too?"

When he turned around to look at me, I noticed his eyes were slightly swollen, the pupils watery. Despite his attempt to remain serious, he stumbled to one side. There could be no doubt: he was drunk.

"It's for Felipe," I answered.

"And why doesn't he buy them himself?"

"He doesn't have any money. He says you owe him."

Leonardo dropped into the chair and put his elbows up on the desk. His head slid slowly between his hands until it hit the wood. He stayed like that for a long time, saying nothing. For a second I thought he was asleep.

"We're in a mess, we're in a mess," he mumbled without lifting his head, his arm stretched out over the desk as if looking for a hold. The first thing he found was a ruler. When he had it in his grip he straightened up to look at it with curiosity. "This is a ruler," he said. "This is a ruler," and dropping it he hopped up vigorously. "Will you come with me? The day after tomorrow we're going to Don Evaristo's estate. We'll talk business: I might have to sell San Gabriel.

VISIONS

*D*espite Ema's warning I kept seeing Leticia, but her presence inspired in me a certain fear. Every time Julia left us alone and Leticia profited to propose one of those games where innocence served pleasure, I participated with so many misgivings and I proved myself so clumsy that Leticia ended up getting angry.

One of those games consisted of awarding me a special prize for each feat I accomplished. When I crossed the creek without taking off my shoes, she let me take her by the waist. If I jumped down from the high branches of the polylepis tree, I could kiss her on the cheek. Swimming a few strokes in the duck lake was an accomplishment she rewarded with a wrestling match, which always finished amid giggles and scratches.

Doubtless tired of always subjecting me to the same trials, Leticia decided to be more demanding. One afternoon, pointing to the viaduct that carried water to the mill, she dared me to walk along its wooden framework. The dare seemed too dangerous to me and I refused categorically.

"So you don't want to?" she exclaimed. "Then you won't know what I was going to give you?"

"What?" I asked, pricked by curiosity.

Leticia went over to Julia and said something to her in secret. The two of them burst out laughing.

"Are you going to do it or not?" said Leticia. "You have time to answer while I count to ten."

When she counted the last number I answered no. It was too late to change my mind. Leticia wounded me with her glance, and turning her back on me she ran off, jumping over clumps of nettles. I sought out Julia's eyes, as if asking for an explanation. The little maid made a gesture of ignorance with her shoulders.

"What did she say to you in your ear?" I interrogated her, grabbing her by the arms.

Since she didn't answer me, I burst into a fit of seigniorial anger. I looked around for something to hit her with. Since I didn't see anything, I lifted an arm and struck her across the cheek with the back of my hand. Right away her legs gave way and she remained on her knees in front of me. I was astounded, almost irritated by that display of humility. Then I ran off toward the viaduct, climbed up the framework, and hung in despair over the gutter until sunset.

I was sure that Leticia would exact some reprisals, but I couldn't imagine what they would be. Early in the morning she would leave for the country with Julia and wouldn't show up until lunch. They must have been walking some strange paths, because every time I went out looking for them I couldn't find them. She would spend the rest of the day putting records on the Victrola or playing cards with Felipe.

Those card games became longer and longer and more and more meaningful. Felipe would pinch her leg with the greatest cheek, availing himself of his authority as an uncle. Leticia merely laughed. I had the impression she was maliciously wooing him. One day I surprised them talking in half-whispers near the gate. When they saw me approaching they went quiet.

To my relief, Felipe had to go up to the mines. A new foreman had arrived one of those days, a sambo with slant eyes and a long scar on his cheek. He brought with him a trace of ocean and coastal dancing. Felipe got drunk with him, had him dance, and was delighted with him. He was a sergeant who had deserted from the army and was wanted by the law, the only explanation for his decision to renounce the coast, palm trees, and confine himself to the bleak Andean plateau.

Taking advantage of Felipe's absence, I tried to approach Leticia. Since she shrank from my advances and turned a deaf ear to my protests, I got angry.

"All right!" I threatened her. "I'll tell you from now on that I'm going to Lima alone. You'll stay here the rest of your life. You'll rot on your farm like Lola!"

Leticia shrugged.

"You're not the only one going to Lima," she answered me. "Felipe's going before you are and he told me he'd take me."

That declaration perturbed me. Not only had she broken her word to keep our trip secret, but she had also chosen Felipe as her confidant, and I didn't trust Felipe at all. His closeness to Leticia made me more and more suspicious. When he came back from the mine the two of them resumed their game. They walked arm in arm through the cloister or they wandered into the orchard for an hour to return with a miserable dozen peaches.

The only reasonable move seemed to me to adapt to his plans. The first chance I had I approached Felipe.

"You asked me a while ago if I wanted to leave San Gabriel with you," I told him. "I told you I didn't want to. But now I've changed my mind. I'm going to go with you two."

Felipe looked puzzled.

"With you two?" he asked.

"Leticia told me she's going to go with you."

"The poor girl fell for it," Felipe repeated, gritting his teeth. Then he turned toward me. "I promised to take her so she she'd stop bothering me. But I'm not going to go with you or her. I need to go alone. Understand?"

I ran immediately to Leticia's bedroom, happy to be able to give her the bad news. I found her sitting on the trunk, a pencil in her hand, in front of a sheet of stationery.

"Felipe's not going to take you!" I sang as I approached her. "Did you hear? He's not going to take you."

She looked up at me as if she didn't understand me. When I repeated the news she made a face of indifference and, without replying, kept working on her letter. I stood there disoriented, watching her writing emerge regularly from the pencil. But looking more closely, I realized all she was doing was drawing deeper and deeper downstrokes. When the paper tore, Leticia stood up and left the room. From the arcades I saw her run across the patio and into Felipe's room. When I got to her side I found her engaged in a thorough job of destruction. She had broken the bottle of pisco that Felipe left on his night table. She took the tube of shaving soap and stamped on it until it burst. Panting, she turned toward me, brushed by, went out the door, and disappeared across the patio.

These fits of rage spoiled her freshness. Nights, she would show up in the living room ashen and with dark circles around her eyes. In a corner of the room, playing solitaire, she excluded herself from the conversations. Felipe speculated about the mess in his room without causing Leticia to start at all. Only when Leonardo told me that at the end of the week we would leave for Don Evaristo's estate did she interrupt her game and go pensive in front of her spread-out cards.

A few days later, one night when we had a visitor—Don Casildo had come to deliver the carpenter's wife's baby—Leticia, who was still withdrawn in her corner, let out a shout and went stiff in her chair. Only after drinking a glass of water could she manage to speak and then she said she had seen a man on the balcony. Then she corrected herself and said it was a woman. In vain did we open the door and scan the road. There wasn't a shadow in sight. When Felipe, who was coming from his room, heard what had happened, he burst out laughing.

"If he had a beard but was wearing a skirt, it must have been a priest!"

Don Casildo spoke of the blessed souls of purgatory. Stories were told. The original motive was forgotten. But since Leticia kept casting anxious glances toward the balcony, Leonardo sent her to bed.

"Let Julia take her mattress in," he said. "That way someone will be with you. And if you feel like it, tomorrow you can come with us to the interior. The trip will be good for you."

In effect, when I went to the stable the next day I found Leticia saddling her mare. Leonardo joined us. The sun, the morning air, the coming trip made us joyful, with one of those wordless joys manifested by sure gestures, by the deftness of your movements. At ten we put the fur pads over the saddles. Five minutes later we were stepping along the great eastern road.

I was soon to suffer a disappointment. As we were going through the town of Mollepata, Leonardo left the road to the interior and took a side road, explaining to me that Don Evaristo wasn't at his property on the lower mountain slopes but at his house on the plateau. I, who had been dreaming about a period of heat and lowland fruits, had to resign myself to that climb through limestone toward the pampas that stung with their air and killed the spirit. So the three of us rode along, almost without talking, until the trees were lost to sight and we came across the first clumps of bunchgrass.

Leticia seemed to love that setting, because she immediately galloped on ahead of us. One after another several flocks of sheep came up to us, doubtless taking us for the salt distributors. A whirlwind of bleating sheep surrounded the horses. The shepherds and the sheep dogs arrived later and pushed the flock away with barks and slaps. Only at dusk did we spot the fence of the ranch house. When we went through the gate, Leticia had already dismounted and was in the patio embracing Don Evaristo' wife.

To the core of an old colonial house, Don Evaristo had added two side wings full of big windows that cried out for ocean and palm trees. The whole was attractive and incoherent. The masons had just finished building a kind of hunting pavilion out back. To the right you could see the mud-brick rooms reserved for the household servants. In one of them there was a crowd of Indians. Don Evaristo said that the night before a shepherd had been struck by lightning.

The drinking started as soon as we went in. In the living room, where a huge stove was burning, were the owner's only two companions: his cook and his veterinarian. Then we went through the house without putting down our glasses, following Don Evaristo, who, full of arrogance, showed us the guest rooms. There were eight in all, each carpeted and heated. Leonardo couldn't hide his envy as he compared that luxury to the damp rooms of San Gabriel.

After a dinner in which the cook, a Swiss man brought from a Lima hotel, took great pains to prepare us strange sauces, the men stayed next to the fire gossiping about the area. Don Evaristo's wife, Leticia, and I went to the next room, where there was a piano. Doña Susana, still dressed like a woman from Lima, as if she were about to go out shopping, talked to us about her children, who were studying in Lima and were going to go to the United States to learn English. Leticia, tipsy from the wine, kept interrupting her to say that she knew English, that she was going to the United States too. When she saw the piano she declared she knew how to play, but that she didn't because it made her sad. For half an hour she spoke without pause, curling up on the sofa, leaping up to walk around the living room, sitting down on the rug, laughing at her own inventions until at last, when Doña Susana, tired by then, said she was going to bed, she went still in her spot, turned off, without light in her pupils, as if stripped of her intelligence.

The two of us remained alone for a long time, face to face, without talking, listening to the oaths and the sound of clinking glasses coming from the room next door. Even though I was tired, I couldn't make up my mind to leave. I was expecting something from Leticia, some reparation after our fight about the viaduct. Finally, she resolved to look at me with a certain curiosity, as if she were amazed her silence hadn't sent me beating a retreat,

"You're still here!" she sighed. "Why don't you go to bed? You barely know how to ride and you must be exhausted.... I've been thinking about lost souls," she added quickly. "I haven't been thinking about anything else for days. Just now, when I was talking, I was thinking about them. Nobody believed me the other day, but it was true that I saw a man on the balcony. He was leaning on the railing as if he'd climbed up a ladder from the road."

After a minute she added:

"That's why I want to leave San Gabriel, because people in San Gabriel suffer in purgatory. Not everybody knows it, of course, but Jacinto does and Alfredo too. That's why Alfredo left."

"There are lost souls in Lima too," I answered.

"But they must be different. Here there are ghosts of dead Indians, of priests too, which are the worst."

"I don't believe that stuff."

"You don't? Look," she said, lowering her voice. "The other night somebody pushed open my door. First some knocks, then the doorknob turned. I turned on the light, but I didn't scream. I waited for whatever it was to come in before I made the sign of the cross. It went away slowly, without rattling chains the way it has other times.... You think that's funny? Of course! You don't understand these things! But one day they'll appear before you and you'll be scared to death. I'm going," she said, getting up. "Come with me to see my room."

I followed her. Halfway down the hall she stopped. When I reached her side I noticed she was disturbed.

"Some days I have a horrible fear," she said quickly. "A fear that lasts weeks and weeks.... I don't know where it could come from. Then it goes away."

Without waiting for my answer, she started walking again. When she got to her room she turned on the light.

"Look under the bed," she said, and as I obeyed she looked through the wardrobe and then out the window to the corrals. "Look!" she suddenly shouted. "There he is! There he is!"

When I ran to the window Leticia pointed to the sheds.

"There! Can't you see? He left. Why didn't you hurry?"

No matter how much I scrutinized the darkness I couldn't see anything. I only heard voices coming from the outbuildings.

"It must have been the watchmen on their rounds."

Leticia sank into thought.

"No. He was there," she replied without conviction.

Then she closed the window and slowly slid the bolt over.

"But I'm not afraid," she added. "It's different here. Nothing will happen here. You can go. I'm going to write a letter tonight."

I hesitated a moment. Then I went to my room. Opening my window, I observed the outbuildings for a long time. The sound of voices kept up. Not long later, Don Evaristo appeared with a lantern in his hand, followed by his guests, to whom he must have been showing the installations. The veterinarian was wearing a white felt hat like those worn by the inhabitants of San Gabriel. Soon after, they disappeared into the darkness.

DESERTION

*I*n San Gabriel there was a bicycle. I discovered it one day while I was prying around the hacienda storerooms. It was when we came back from the high plateau. The crops had ripened, borne all their fruit, and the fields lay open, exhausted, and livid, waiting for the fallow season.

It was strange to see a bicycle there, see it where there were no flat roads. Even so, I gave it to Reynaldo to fix for me, and when it was ready I had a good time riding over the flagstones of the cloister.

Jacinto, enthused by my find, immediately wanted to imitate me, and together with him I set off along rugged roads, up hills, crashing, bursting inner tubes, but in the end he learned to ride and became an expert cyclist. All by himself he went on long rides for which, obeying Lord knows what singular idea of the art of bicycle riding, he would put on his three-piece Sunday suit.

It was also around then that Don Evaristo's people came. They came to cut the four hundred eucalyptus trees that Leonardo had sold him. Felipe went to the grove several times to watch them working. They made firewood from the trunks. Others they took away whole for the dam their boss was building. They carried them through the gorges with the strength of their hands, like ants dragging a caterpillar.

Having received his pay, Felipe started packing. When his bags were ready and we were all expecting to see him leave, a kind of apathy came over him, and still dressed in his traveling clothes he could be seen pacing the arcades with that disconcerted, puzzled, incredulous, slightly idiotic, and irremediably comic look of someone who has just missed a train. In the end he shut himself in his room and started to drink and pay for the hacienda beer. Leonardo said that at that rate he wouldn't even make it to Santiago. At night, he would call for Jacinto, the servant Jisha, or me and give us money.

"I need to spend," he would say. "But since there's nothing to buy in San Gabriel, I give the money away. Have a good time, kids! Go blow it all!"

The only one bothered by this was Aunt Ema. She sometimes came into the room when we were all there having a big party, and kicking us out she would remain alone with Felipe. From behind the screen I heard her scolding him, urging him to leave immediately, or to give her his money so she could keep it for him.

But Felipe didn't let himself be tamed. Precisely during that fit of extravagance, he sent Jacinto one afternoon to Mollepata to bring back some bottles of champagne. Jacinto insisted on going by bike even though the road was muddy. We waited for him until it got dark and we were just getting ready to go out looking for him when the Indians from the community of Urcos showed up carrying him. He had crashed going down a hill and broken his ankle. They were also carrying the carcass of the bicycle.

The first idea was to take him to Santiago, then to telegraph the town doctor, later to appeal to Don Casildo for help; finally, it was Tobías, the carpenter, who, like someone fixing the leg of a table, set the bone in its place.

The one who thundered most in the middle of this bustle was Felipe, not because of Jacinto or the bicycle, but because of his champagne. Since the only person responsible for it was injured and he couldn't take it out on him, he declared that a *sol* had disappeared from his night table and he blamed the misdeed on Jisha. Felipe dragged him up to the loft, tied his hands with a rope, and hung him from one of the roof-beams. Five minutes later, bored or repentant, he let him go and sent him away with a kick in the rear.

That's how the days went by in San Gabriel, the days of the last summer rains. Small and large miseries followed one another. They were interesting one day, boring another, not very moving, they taught nothing, and infallibly they ended up being forgotten.

But Father Argensolas's arrival was an event of some resonance. One morning he showed up on a beautiful mare. When, saddlebags over his shoulders, he dismounted and walked toward the arcades, his bearing impressed us. He was unusually tall for someone from the highlands. He was, in addition, white, with a deeply receding hairline, and two slanting blue eyes that seemed to be constantly scrutinizing something behind us, behind the walls.

The first thing to surprise us was his way of shaking hands. His fingers barely brushed ours before escaping as if under the effect of an electric shock. Sitting in a living room armchair, he would talk for hours about trifles, about the weather, the road, avoiding concrete answers and deliberately creating an air of mystery around himself. It was only during lunch that he admitted he was traveling to Lima, since he had been summoned by a well-known character for certain "secret consultations."

Then we found out he was a magician and a devotee of the occult. He said he had accomplished all kinds of wonders, from curing deadly diseases to finding lost people and belongings.

"It's neither the work of God nor of the devil," he said, "but only the exercise of my mental faculties."

Even though he didn't touch a drop of liquor, he reached a state of excitation as he talked and smoked that was very near drunkenness. He spoke of a goddaughter of his who could move objects from a distance and who, under his direction, would soon acquire the gift of ubiquity. He said, at last, that if he wanted to he could see the Pope right then.

His declaration astounded us. Pressured most of all by the women, he agreed to effect that marvel. We all went to the living room. Father Argensolas sat in an armchair and we gathered around him. Then he ordered that the curtains be closed, stretched his arms out, and started gazing at the palms of his hands. His face took on the features of extreme attention. His long and bony fingers opened and closed.

"It's necessary to concentrate," he said. "All that needs to happen for the phenomenon to fail is for one of you to lose interest."

In effect, nearly imperceptible beams were emanating from his fingers, as if an electric current was flowing between his hands. Meanwhile, the priest described what he was seeing: the Pope in the Council of Cardinals, his vestments, the Roman decor. When he finished, Ema declared that she had seen a miter. Felipe burst out laughing.

The priest looked at him sarcastically.

"You think I'm a fraud? Of course, you're a materialist and you worship only what's within reach of your senses. I know what you like: women and brandy."

Felipe's expression changed.

"So that you don't take me for a charlatan," the priest continued, "I'll tell you your future."

Felipe accepted willingly. The tension the priest had created had grown, Leticia hadn't opened her mouth the whole time, and was following the gestures and picking up every one of the visitor's words with unshakable conviction.

"One thing though," added the priest. "I need a moment of concentration. Do you have a quiet room? I'll rest for a few minutes."

Leonardo led him to one of the guest rooms. Ten minutes later the priest reappeared. Stretching out in one of the armchairs in the living room, he opened his mouth.

"You have a big job to do. You could become a millionaire if you use good judgment. But working in the highlands doesn't bring in much unless you have a lot of capital. What's more, you will soon commit an act of disloyalty. In short, I see only failure. I'm very sorry. That's all I know."

The priest went quiet. Felipe didn't dare contradict him. It was

Leonardo who, I don't know why, since he was as unbelieving as Felipe, decided to ask him about Leticia's visions. For a few minutes the priest looked absent-mindedly at Leticia as he talked about other things, as if he hadn't heard Leonardo's request. Finally, he stood up, took her by the shoulders, and stared into her eyes. He was looking at her that way for a long time, while we remained in suspense. At last he let her go:

"Very odd!" he said. "But it's nothing that's not human."

"What?" asked Leonardo.

"Nothing, nothing. You'll know yourself soon enough."

No matter how much he insisted, the priest wouldn't explain his reply. He said he was exhausted and went off to go to sleep. He left the next morning. We couldn't forget his eyes, his cassock, or his look of a mad prodigy. He was doubtless a deluxe fraud, but in his hands he had at least a thread of truth

Soon after, Felipe told us he was leaving. From then on everything in the hacienda changed. An outsider wouldn't have noticed anything, but for me the stars had a different gleam. By dint of watching them, I had recognized their language. A sidereal voice came from out of the blue.

It was one evening. Felipe said:

"I'm leaving this morning at three. I'll say goodbye to everyone before dinner because I'll be arranging my things afterward."

At ten at night Felipe embraced everyone and went to his room. We stayed in the living room. A record was immediately put on. I danced with Leticia and noticed that she was distracted, different. Here movements were clumsy and her arms weighed heavily on my shoulders. Her hair was slightly messy and it gave off a kind of perfume of funeral flowers.

"You're sad," I said to her.

"It's true," she replied. "But it doesn't matter."

That was all. I went to bed around midnight. Felipe, in his side, was arranging his things for the hundredth time. Then he went out to the stable to saddle his horse. Hours went by. I probably had a short and dreamless sleep. The whinnying of a horse woke me up around dawn. From my bed I heard hoofbeats going off toward the gate. Felipe was leaving…. Would I ever see him again?

With a leap I rushed to the window to gaze at his silhouette setting off on that trip that promised such good fortune. Pulling the sheer curtain open, I saw the country, the swift sorrel-colored horse that Felipe was leading by the bridle. A second horse appeared. I recognized it immediately: it was Aunt Ema's. She herself was riding it, wrapped in her blue shawl, her white hat pulled down over her forehead. They both spurred their mounts and rode out at a smooth trot toward Santiago.

Under the effect of incredulity I opened the window and leaned half my body out over the ledge. It was freezing. Their silhouettes, going around a bend in the road, were barely visible. A light came on in one of the balconies of the house. Leonardo, leaning on the railing, had lit a cigarette and was blowing out the first mouthful of smoke over the now deserted road.

THE STING

At first there was an attempt to cover up the desertion. Leonardo said that Ema had been obliged to leave suddenly for Santiago to help Aunt Mabila, who was ill. The servants believed it, Leticia, too, but the gringa María, far from falling for the deception, started making a show of incredulity. Every time Leonardo, in full possession of his lie by then, embellished it by giving it new forms, she maliciously sought our gaze, laughed to herself, and poured herself large glasses of chicha that she gulped down, satisfied with her subtleties in her role as the silent informer.

The act didn't last long. Leonardo suddenly stopped talking about Ema and Mabila. Meals became slow and silent. That long table once full of shouts and battles seemed extraordinarily sad. One day María deliberately took the fugitive's seat. That act spoke for itself. When we saw her sitting there we realized there was nothing to hope for anymore. With the breach closed, everything went back to normal.

I wandered through the labyrinths of the house, wavering, discouraged. I thought that nothing could keep me in San Gabriel, not the people, not the places. With the summer gone, everything had fallen into a profound autumnal melancholy. In the mountains the seasons had a deep and doleful truth. Everything was full of dead vegetables, and even the very dirt of the house, the furniture, the patio, seemed like dying dust.

In the meantime, through a slow and successive gradation of gestures, Leticia was taking on an expression of stupor, of absolute estrangement from life. Maybe she had found out about everything, maybe her visions had started up again. But we didn't know anything. In the big fig tree in the orchard, where some early figs were hanging, pecked at by birds, she had set up her residence, her aerial, unreachable world. When I went around there with Jacinto to hunt doves, we would see her up high, straddling a branch, her gaze fixed on the horizon.

"Leticia!" we shouted at her. "Leticia!"

She pretended not to see us, and if we insisted she spit on us or threw rotten figs at us.

"Something's happening to that girl," Leonardo said. And his entire tutelage was limited to that observation.

Don Evaristo's people had finished felling the wood. Leonardo would walk around the stumps of his trees with his riding crop in his hand. He said he would plant new eucalyptus trees in the hill with the viaduct and had already started recruiting people in the villages. He met with recruiters, argued, and then went out drinking in the nearby way-side inns. Sometimes he would bring in an Indian woman who ate in the kitchen and stayed at the hacienda for a week before disappearing without a trace. María harassed these women behind Leonardo's back. The Indian women stopped coming. María's presence in hacienda affairs was becoming more and more noticeable. In the end, after having reigned over Leonardo's solitude, she reigned over San Gabriel.

One evening, Don Evaristo and his wife appeared. Even though Leonardo had sworn not to take in any more guests, they had to be welcomed. Euphoric, Don Evaristo told about his discovery of his lands on the mountain slopes. Thousands of hectares that he had never seen, that this time, guided by his foreman, he had traversed to their hottest boundaries.

"That won't be touched until my children are older," he said. "Great for them! If they make it work for them they'll eat off gold tableware."

That prosperity seemed to hurt Leonardo, who remained taciturn for the whole visit. The evening before his departure, Don Evaristo took a sudden interest in inspecting the pastures, the accounts, the equipment. He, who was slow and talkative, became an active man, bothersome and succinct in his inspection. In the end he remained skeptical. Only his wife seemed to understand him.

"Nice land," he said, scratching his chin. "Sheltered land for good alfalfa."

"Nice land!" repeated Leonardo when his guest left. "Now I know what that lizard wants! But I'll divide it among my sharecroppers first."

"He's become envious," the gringa would say, pointing to Leonardo. In his place I'd sell San Gabriel and move to Lima. Here the lice are going to eat us up. It's past time to live like civilized people."

Leonardo might have been thinking the same thing, because his desk was covered with clippings from Lima newspapers advertising houses and farms on the coast. But out of stubbornness, pride, or sheer love, he insisted on staying in a house that was falling to pieces and on land that had offered neither harvesters nor plowmen. When he went through the cloisters with his long beard and his wild eyes, his figure took on something ghostly and I started thinking he had a vague resemblance to Jacinto.

To avoid these evil apparitions, I started wandering around the country again. Following the river, I had discovered a waterfall where I bathed alone, letting out cries of joy. Then I would chase the water skeeters and destroy them by bombing them with stones or I would climb up the bluffs to reach wild blackberries. I often went to visit Don Casildo, who offered me chicha and told me fabulous stories where the animals were intelligent and even the rocks talked. Then I went with him through the ravines where he gathered medicinal herbs.

On my way back from one of those outings, I spotted Leticia's green pullover. Approaching from behind her on tiptoe, I got to her side and let out a shout. She turned swiftly around and when she saw me—she was smoking—she threw the butt to the ground and started laughing. Nitucha, one of the carpenter's daughters, emerged as if by magic from the entrails of the earth. We were next to that natural fissure we had discovered on the deer hunt. I realized just then that Leticia's laughter was nervous.

"Idiot! You could have killed me!" she exclaimed, getting up. "Where are you coming from?"

"From Don Casildo's"

She observed me from head to toe with surprise.

"From the witch doctor's," she repeated. "Are you sick or something?"

"No, it's just that he's the only interesting person in San Gabriel."

Leticia cast a quick glance at me and sat down again.

"I was watching the ants," she said. "Have you seen?" she pointed to a line of traveling ants that formed a black trace on the ground. "I've been watching them for a while. They come and go like crazy. I don't know why! Sometimes two meet, greet each other, and start talking."

"And what's Nitucha doing down there?"

"I sent her to look for the anthill."

Leaning over the edge, I saw the ants penetrating the fissure and disappearing into the depths. I was starting to get interested in that long animal migration when I heard Leticia's voice coming from behind me.

"Ants are so boring!"

When I turned around I saw her rubbing her eyes as if to get rid of a used-up expression.

"And you think I come here to look at ants?"

"Then what for?"

Standing up, she signaled for me to follow her and led me along the fissure to a place where it got wider, opening a terrible and damp mouth that caused a violent contraction in your stomach when you looked at it.

"I sometimes stand here," she said. "I stand on the very edge, close my eyes, and say: 'If I took only one step, if the wind pushed me....'"

"You're crazy!" I said, furiously leaving her side.

Leticia chased me, jumped around me.

"It's just a game!" she was saying. "A game!"

I pushed her away with my hand and she let herself go without putting up resistance, spun around a few times, and ended up looking shy, hurt, with the expression of a sad and defenseless animal. Intrigued, I approached her.

"I should cry," she said, holding out her bloodless and twitching hands. "Something made me feel cold."

"It's your stupid games," I told her. "Let's go back home," and I started walking away.

She followed me without protesting, her arms crossed over her breast as if she were shivering. Behind her Nitucha was running along and amusing herself among the fields of prickly pear. Finally, some locals were, by chance, going our way. Turning around now and then, I realized that we formed a line like the ants, a longer and longer line that was rushing blindly into the evening depths.

When we made it to the hacienda, Leticia lay down and had herself served spearmint tea. I found out from Nitucha that she was having dizzy spells because of the fissure. I thought that she was faking it or that a scorpion or some poisonous spider might have gotten to her. At night, she sent for Leonardo. María and I waited in the living room, silent, because it was precisely loneliness that separated us. Only when Leonardo came back did she decide to open her mouth.

"Everybody is sickly here," she said. "I don't know what's happening to them. Just breathing the air they get poisoned."

"Leticia wants to go to Aunt Mabila's!" exclaimed Leonardo. "Great idea! The old woman spoils her. The poor girl is dying of boredom here."

In effect, two days later, Leticia, having gotten over her spell of weakness, got ready to ride to Santiago. I was a little annoyed because she hadn't asked me to go with her. Even though Leonardo asked me later if I wanted to go, I refused out of tact, fearing Leticia would be against it. It was Jacinto who would go with her, and from early in the morning he was walking around overjoyed, exercising his horse on the patio, shouting every time it reared near the arches of the arcades that he'd go to the cinema in Santiago and that when he came back he'd tell me about the movie.

The two of them left at noon. I ran behind them until the climb. There they stopped for a moment, as horsemen usually did, to look at the hollow and the hacienda. Leticia observed it all without emotion, shivering in the cold, and when she spurred her horse to set off again, she gave me a strange wave of the hand, a wave that was neither farewell nor see you later, but something like a sign of annoyance, renunciation, or the absolute negation of everything left behind her.

The telegram came exactly twenty-four hours later. It was brought by a man who rode from Mollepata. He must have received precise instructions, because he came into the living room where we were having lunch and delivered it personally to Leonardo. My uncle read it several times and in the end he folded it and put it under his plate. He tried to go on eating as though nothing had happened, but all at once he got up, noisily flung his chair away, and left in a rush without any explanation at all.

The gringa made a gesture of indifference, and taking a chewed-up piece of meat out of her mouth she reached over to pick up the telegram. After reading it, she murmured sententiously:

"Bad news always comes at mealtime."

I left my seat and ran out. When I got to the patio I saw Leonardo hauling a saddle over to the stables. When I caught up with him he was already next to Chicuelo, tightening the cinches.

"I'll go with you!" was all I managed to say to him.

"What does all this matter to you?" he replied angrily. "You're just getting yourself mixed up in other people's troubles."

"Is something wrong with Leticia?"

His only answer was a gesture of impatience.

The only available horse was María's white mare, a cunning beast, and so old that grandmother Marica had taken her last rides on it. I saddled her quickly, and as I went out the stable gate to the road Leonardo, without looking back, was already making his way up the hill.

For an hour I followed him without seeing a trace of him, without even knowing if I was going the right way. Only when I descended to the first stream did I see him, waiting in front of a bridge.

"You can't go across it!" he yelled to me, letting me know with a gesture that I should follow him.

We forded the stream. When we got to Angasmarca we dismounted for a cup of black coffee. The big rock that buttressed the Algallama pampas and looked like a gigantic miter reminded me of my trip through that place barely a year ago. I went the rest of the way harried by a series of confusing thoughts. I stopped worrying about Leticia. I told myself that in mounting the mare all I was trying to do was to become an actor in an adventure that didn't concern me, participate in a funeral party that nothing other than my selfish curiosity for other people's disgraces invited me to.

Night was falling when we finished crossing the pampas. On the other side of the valley you could see a kind of sad, scattered galaxy: the lights of Santiago. Just before midnight we went in on the main street of the town and stopped at the Hotel Santa María to reserve a room. Then we went on to see Mabila, who lived in the outskirts, close to the cemetery.

We went through the gate without dismounting. We saw Ollanta holding a lantern in the foyer, then Jacinto, who came out to welcome us rubbing his hands together. We went into a big living room, full of old furniture and lighted candles whose light was reflected in filmy mirrors. Mabila was there, wrapped in her shawl with a long knotted fringe. I dropped into a sofa that creaked and almost broke. Mabila and Leonardo went to the inner rooms. Jacinto brought me a glass of punch and took me right away to eat in the kitchen.

As I used my hands to devour several fried and burned sweet potatoes, Jacinto vented his feelings:

"I haven't even had time to go to the stadium! The whole time running from one place to another!"

"Tell me what's going on," I menaced him.

"Don't you know? I don't know what's with that girl! Yesterday, when we were in the Cachicadán ravine, she started feeling bad. Going up, she was as green as a lime and could barely stay in the saddle. It was just as well that we were already close, because she fell off just as we made it to Santiago. Blood was spurting out of her; her trousers were all black."

"It's a hemorrhage," added Ollanta, who was wandering around the cookstove. "Aunt Mabila says that's what she gets for riding a horse 'in her condition.'"

Jacinto added something, but I didn't catch it. Ollanta's words had hurt me like a shot to the temple. Everything was buzzing and writhing around me. I got up and left the kitchen, then the house, I walked around the market streets, around the treeless main square covered with rickety vegetation. When I got to the Hotel Santa María I asked for the room key and threw myself into bed without undressing.

I must have slept almost twenty-four hours, because when I woke up the next day it was already dark. Leonardo was looking in his suitcase for his pajamas and when he saw me he asked if I was sick. Since I was hungry, I went down to eat something at the bar where the town notables shot pool.

When I went up, Leonardo was in bed, shielding himself from the light bulb with a hand over his eyes. Since he seemed to me approachable and forsaken, I asked him to pay me what he owed me from the mine, or just enough to get to Lima.

"You're leaving?" he asked me with indifference.

The next day he gave me two hundred *soles*.

"You'll have to go see Leticia," he said to me.

I just shrugged.

"She's very weak,..." he added. "She's really sick. If she doesn't get better we'll have to take her to Trujillo."

I went with him to Mabila's house. There I said goodbye to Jacinto, who did everything he could to get me to stay.

"Who am I going to talk to?" he said to me. "At least stay until tomorrow! That way we can go to the movies tonight."

Refusing, I asked him come with me into Leticia's room.

We went through the darkened living room, with its smell of dead moths and damp. In the doorway I stopped short and didn't dare enter. I was sure that entering that hazy bedroom was all it would take for me to fall into Leticia's world again, that strange world full of lies and tricks, ablutions and games, which now seemed to me bloody games.

"I'm leaving," I said, turning on my heels.

In the hall I ran into Leonardo on his way to the bank. He went with me to a travel agency. Without baggage, I got into a truck that left half an hour later. As we left Santiago and started going through that red and soapy land, I struggled not to think about San Gabriel, where everything was leading me. I had the feeling that something of mine had been left there for good, a way of life maybe, or a fate that I had renounced so I could take away and save more purely my testimony. Only when we passed the Quiruvilca mines and the truck started going down did I realize we were getting close to the coast. Then I didn't think anymore about anything but the ocean, its vast empty beaches bitten by the waters in slow and foamy mouthfuls.

Glossary

Chicha – Traditional Andean beverage made from fermented or unfermented corn.

Huayno – Popular music and dance of the Andes.

Pachamanca – Traditional Andean method of roasting meat and tubers among hot stones.

Pisco – The brandy distilled from a white grape grown in Peru and Chile.

Pishtaco – A malevolent outsider (imaginary) who haunts the northern highlands of Peru in search of Indian children to suck the fat out of, which fat was reputed to go into the making of church bells, or more recently, to have been sold to reduce the foreign debt.

Sol – Peru's unit of currency until 1985, when it was replaced by the *inti.* The Peruvian pound, established in 1931, was worth ten *soles* and was the equivalent of the British pound. In 1991 the *inti* was retired and the *sol,* now known as the *nuevo sol,* was reintroduced.

Viscacha – A large South American rodent that looks like a long-tailed rabbit.